Electa
A Historical Novel

by

Dennis W. Fabel

ISBN: 0-7596-7920-7

249 S. Beechgrove Rd.
Wilmington, Ohio, 45177
(937) 383-5727

1stBooks - rev. 3/18/02

A Word of Appreciation

I must thank my wife Carolyn for her support, ideas, and for listening to my frequent ramblings about this book for the last seven years. Mark Weber and Louis Schmittroth; thank you for your encouragement. If I were wiser and had more time, I would have taken advantage of your kind offers to help. I appreciate Brien Jones of 1stBooks Library, who stood ready to help as this project neared completion. Last but not least, many thanks to Angela Fabel, for her encouragement, excitement, and editing skills, without which this work would still be a dream.

Chapter One ~ Away on the *Emilie*

On the steamship *Emilie's* deck, a small crowd gathered around James Vail and his family: his wife Martha, young son, and daughter, and sister-in-law Electa Bryan. A large bearded man wearing moccasins, leather pants over sweat-stained red long johns, and a round-brimmed gray hat stepped forward to confront James.

"You're goin' to the mountains to do what?" the man demanded in a raspy voice.

"To teach Indians at a government farm on Sun River. I must convince them that they have to learn how to farm."

"I've been in the Rockies ten winters and I say it can't be done," the disgusted man said. "And where you're goin' the Blackfeet are the worst. I know. Why don't you shoot 'em instead?" he said, and a few other rough-looking men laughed.

"Your cruelty degrades even your humor," James replied clearly yet quietly.

"They deserve it," the man challenged, stepping closer.

Electa's homespun gray dress, which matched her gray eyes, stood out noticeably in the crowd since few white women had been to Fort Benton. She wasn't quite as tall as her sister Martha. Electa held a blue parasol up as a shield from the sun. She usually kept a mother-of-pearl comb placed neatly in her blonde shoulder-length hair. She had quietly listened, but typically spoke her mind, especially when asked. So she decided that she had heard enough, and turned to face the men who became suddenly silent. She spoke softly yet firmly.

"James, the lust for gold has blinded these men to higher things. We cannot expect them to understand our calling, nor our compassion for the Indians." Her calm demeanor and quiet, smooth voice seemed to relax the men, who looked at each other, somewhat surprised.

"Gentlemen," she said, "we are going west for different reasons, so perhaps we shouldn't dispute one another, since we might face great hardship together. I suggest that you mind your affairs and let us mind ours." She had faced another fear, this time suddenly and without much forethought. How dare these people question their mission? Months of prayer braced her with enough courage to leave Ohio. To remain behind was unthinkable. After all, she had never lived apart from Martha, not in all her twenty years.

"Say, mister, are you a federal agent?" a man said.

"In a way. An Indian agent hired me. By the way, I also hope to start a school where my sister-in-law, Miss Electa Bryan, will teach," he said, placing his hand under her elbow to introduce her.

The man frowned at her but tipped his hat and said, "You're takin' on a mighty big job that won't work nohow."

"With hard work, patience, perseverance, and the Lord's help, much can be done," James said firmly. A schoolteacher and farmer with black hair and mustache, James's lean, tall yet brawny frame had been built by a lifetime of labor. He smiled at the curiosity seekers gathered around them. There was nothing he could do about the attention since a story about their mission had appeared in newspapers. The War Between the States had begun just over a year earlier. Some rallied around Old Glory, Abe Lincoln, and one nation under God. Others felt states' rights should come first, and many had only self-interest in mind. The voices around him raised, strained loudly with emotion.

"How can you run a farm and a school at the same time? You're only one man."

"Why do Injuns need to read and write? I can't."

"It's plumb crazy to teach Indians how to cipher."

"Aren't you afraid what them Injuns will do to your family?"

Seeing disgust and anger in their eyes he decided to try and explain. "I am not afraid for my family's safety because God will protect us. The Indians must learn how to farm or they won't survive."

The *Emilie*, prepared to leave St. Louis on May 14, 1862, was one of a dozen steamships lined up in the wide Mississippi. She would be the first side-wheeled steamship to take goldseekers to Fort Benton, Dakota Territory. Roustabouts stowed cargo on her main deck, where the engines made it the hottest place onboard. Most of the passengers climbed stairs to the cooler hurricane deck where they could see better and perhaps wave goodbye. At the captain's command, water began churning through her large paddles, pushing her white bulk over the water and her passengers into their future. Black plumes spewed from her tall smokestacks while a whistle wailed a long proud blast. James placed an arm around his wife, Martha. Her auburn hair glistened in the sun as it flowed from beneath her bonnet, and their eyes met as lover's eyes do. Mary, who was four, and little Harvey, only two, stood backed into their mother's homespun blue dress staring up at the strangers with wide, innocent brown eyes they had inherited from their mother. The large man spoke again, this time for the benefit of the crowd and himself.

"They're crazy for trying that," he said, shaking his head.

"And the government is plum crazy to send them," another voice added.

In frustration, the man turned to James and rasped out a final declaration. "Mister, I don't care if Injuns survive or not. That's the craziest thing I ever did hear. If you're smart you'll see the elephant and head to the diggin's with the rest of us, and forget about learnin' them varmints how to farm."

The crowd dispersed except for a tall, young, blonde man with muttonchop sideburns, who approached James. Electa noticed his easy smile and blue eyes. He wore a white shirt over broad shoulders, tucked neatly into black pantaloons.

"Excuse me sir," the man said, "but there is someone here who believes in your cause. I'm Francis Thompson. I work for a mining company, but I respect your mission and admire your courage." He turned to Electa, touched the brim of his hat and said, "And such boldness in a lady is refreshing."

"Sir, I assure you, Mr. Thompson, is it?" she said, blushing.

"Francis Thompson, but please call me Francis."

"How do you do? Mr. Thompson, we didn't ask to be faced by so much doubt. Please excuse me while I find my room. Martha, will you join me?"

The women each took a child and walked away. James leaned against the railing, smiled, and looked at the man, who returned his grin. "Electa can be forward by nature," he said. "But thank you for your kindness, Mr. Thompson. Will you join us for dinner?"

"I would be honored," Francis said. "I'll meet you in the Promenade at six."

That evening, James led his family to the Grand Salon that ran almost the entire length of the ship. Upon entering, Martha was awestruck. Electa gasped and whispered, "My lands, have you ever seen such a place?"

Snow-white tablecloths and napkins, gleaming glasses, shining silverware, and fresh flowers greeted them, adorning every table. Burgundy drapes with gold fringe hung on the walls between tall mirrors the entire length of the room. Ornate white carvings with gold trim decorated the ceiling, and under it all was a fine burgundy carpet. Black waiters in white jackets seated everyone. The Vails were seated at a wall table.

James grinned and said, "Isn't it fine?" He stood to shake their guest's hand when he approached their table. "Mr. Thompson, thank you for coming. Please sit down. You recall my wife Martha, and sister-in-law, Electa Bryan?"

"Of course. Ladies, I am honored."

Martha returned his smile while Electa looked at her plate and blushed again. He placed his hand on the back of the chair beside Electa's. "May I, Miss Bryan?"

She replied with a slight nod. After their food was served, James prayed. "Dear God, thank You for this food which smells so wonderful, and this beautiful room to enjoy Your bountiful grace. Thank You for our new friend, and may You bless our journey. Grant us safety as we travel to our new home. In Jesus' name, amen."

Men at nearby tables noticed. Some just stared, while others had joined the prayer by silently bowing their heads. One young man wearing Confederate gray woolen pants spoke up with a distinctly southern sound. "Well, the Yank ain't just a schoolmarm, he's a preacher too," he said.

His friends laughed. Evidently the tables were as divided as the nation.

"So, you've brought the war with you? All right, Reb," another man said while beginning to move toward the southerner.

"Never mind that!" said a loud voice from the doorway. Captain La Barge's stocky frame presented a commanding figure in his standard black suit and bow tie. A white shirt matched his neatly trimmed beard. Two men carrying rifles stood behind him. "If you'd rather fight than look for gold, then you should have stayed and fought! Any man who incites violence or fights on my ship will be taken to shore at once."

"Excuse me, Captain, may I say something?" James said, standing up.

"Yes, Mr. Vail?"

"Gentlemen, we're all here for our own reasons. Let us leave the war behind and agree to disagree on the matters of North and South. And let's not allow our differences to jeopardize our undertaking, whatever it may be."

After looking at one another, the men sat down. The tension seemed to fade.

"Well said, Mr. Vail. That had better be the last of that, or I will have the last word," the captain said, and he and his men left the room.

"Let's eat before our food gets cold," Martha said, breaking the silence. She and Electa served the children first, and then themselves. It was the first fine meal together of many. Before them sat fried chicken, beef dodgers, succotash, brown betty pudding, gingersnaps, and tea.

"Mr. Thompson, have you traveled this far on a steamship before?" James asked.

"No, I haven't, and I must admit that I never thought about the men who sleep on the decks. You have to watch where you walk at night for fear of stepping on them."

They all laughed at the thought.

"I hope that we're amused at such a comedy and not their misfortune," Martha said. "I'm thankful that the government has provided for our fare or we wouldn't be able to afford cabins either. Dear, how many passengers are there?"

James wiped his mouth with a napkin. "I believe that the passenger list has a total of eighty-five cabin passengers and fifty-three more who rent space on the decks. Quite a crowd for a month-long trip. By the way, ladies, please stay in your cabins after dusk if possible. You might step on someone," he added with an impish smile.

They laughed again, glad to have a good-natured spirit at their table at least.

"Let us drink a toast to new friends, a safe journey, and life in the West," Francis said, lifting his glass. "Only the good Lord knows what adventures we'll face."

After sipping his river water, James said, "Thank you. It was only after much prayer that we made the difficult decision to go to the wilderness, but we trust that God will see us through to Sun River Farm."

"I never dreamed we would be on such a ship," Martha said. I'm so excited that I hope I can sleep."

Electa smiled politely, but said nothing. After dinner Mr. Thompson excused himself and the Vails went to their cramped cabins to rest. Martha put Harvey and Mary to bed while Electa wrote to a friend back home.

~

Dear Victoria,   May 14, 1862

I hope this finds you in good health. We are all well. I am excited but miss you and our beloved home. While on the Ohio I felt some nearness to you, but now that we are faraway, I am, as Martha says, "homesick," which is a good name for it. We pray together often. The men on the ship are quite rough and there are more than one hundred thirty-five of them. Remember when we spoke of my possibly finding a husband in the West? I doubt that will happen if this lot is the best there is, since I refuse to wed an ungodly man. Perhaps Sunday worship will reveal more believers than I realize.

Pray that the good Lord will somehow heal the ache in my heart for home. I now understand the saying, "Home is where the heart is," for mine breaks apart more each day and with each passing mile. I am afraid that I left one half of my heart behind and that it will always be there, waiting for me. Yet I don't know when, if ever, I shall return. I will post this at the first opportunity. Devotedly yours,

Electa Bryan

Chapter Two ~ Buffaloes and Indians

One week later, Electa, Martha, and the children sat on blankets in the warm sun as the green landscape slowly slid by. The *Emilie* left her endless black trail in the blue sky.

"You know I would go anywhere with you," Electa said, "but dreaming of the West is so different than going! These windstorms that force us to stop scare me almost to death. Yet I'm mystified that I'm becoming more excited."

"Well, you've always had the wanderlust," Martha teased.

During that first week their routine had settled into meals, walks around the decks, and caring for Mary and Harvey. They talked mostly of the children and their new home. While the children played on the blanket with toys, Electa watched the treed shoreline pass and breathed in the muddy smell of the river. The sun flashed on the water, making her squint. Her brow became a furrow of thought.

"What we're doing is a fearsome thing," she said, "but there is no turning back. God is with us, and we have one another as always, so we must be brave or else place a great weight on James."

"Yes, of course," Martha said, producing courage with a smile. "Let's keep praying, and determine that nothing shall discourage us."

Looking up the river ahead they could see only a short distance, and then what? Suddenly, Electa noticed an enormous cloud of dust beyond the trees upriver. "Look at that strange cloud," she said, shielding her eyes from the sun. "What could it be?"

Martha's courage faded as fear welled up within her like the brown billowing clouds she saw. As calmly as possible she said, "Please find James and have him come see it." As Electa rose to leave she added, "And pray!"

A man with leathery brown skin leaned against a nearby railing. He wore a floppy hat, out from which his long hair ruffled in the breeze, and he smelled of sweat and greasy buckskin. Pointing the stem of his pipe at the green hills he shouted, "Look! On the hills! Buff!" He laughed heartily. "Fresh meat tonight! You pilgrims are in for a certain sure treat."

The news spread throughout the ship as it drew closer and many gathered to see the brown beasts. Men hurriedly retrieved their guns. James and Electa made their way through the crowd and found Martha.

"My dear, what is it; what's wrong?" James asked.

The buckskin-clad man interrupted, "There ain't nothin' wrong, mister, lessen you don't like fresh meat."

James introduced his family and found that the man's name was Carter.

"But what is that brown cloud?" Martha asked.

James looked at the buffalo and said, "My dear, it must be the dust from a large herd."

"Yore right about that, mister," Carter said. "Lady, it takes lots of buff to kick up a big fuss like that. We'll see Injuns long about now too, I reckon. They follow buffler for supplies."

The *Emilie* soon entered a turn in the river's course.

"Look at that wonder!" Electa said.

An enormous brown form seemed to crawl across the river as the brown beasts moved from one shore to the other. The pilot, ever alert and fearing damage to the ship, slowed to a crawl, sliding her as gently as possible into the mass of hairy, swimming flesh. Wide, white eyes set in shaggy brown fur surrounded the steamship. Many of the grunting, panting animal's horns knocked against her sides. Gunshots and excited shouts began to ring out. Men roped and then pulled dead and dying, dripping wet buffalo up onto the deck. One man amazed Electa by pulling a live calf out of the water. Both it and the man stood on the deck soaking wet and breathing heavily.

"Why capture a wild animal, and on a ship?" she wondered out loud.

Standing beside her, James said, "I don't believe that Captain La Barge would ever allow that."

"And what will you be doing with a live animal aboard?" the captain, arms crossed, demanded of the man.

"It will make a fine pet!" he replied, but the wild youngster gained its breath, panicked, and charged, scrambling the crowd in every direction.

"Shoot that animal before someone gets hurt!" shouted the captain. A shot rang out. Electa gasped, covering her face with her hands. "Besides, a calf will taste better than those giants," he said.

Men continued to shout while guns boomed. The pungent odor of wet buffalo joined with the scent of the river and the dirty smell of burning black powder. James went to their cabin to be with his family. There, he embraced Martha as he noticed how the walls muffled the violent sounds. Martha took a deep breath, closed her eyes, and rested her head on his shoulder. "It's all right, dear, we are quite safe," he said.

"I didn't know how safe we were out there," she said, "and the children didn't need to see that. I suppose we'll have the animals for dinner. I'm sure the good Lord doesn't want His supply of fresh meat wasted. We should be thankful."

Several days later, true to Carter's prediction, nervous passengers saw Indians on horseback keeping up with the *Emilie*. Other Indians waited for the ship at a point where the river narrowed. When the ship appeared, one of them rode into the water and waved his arms. Carter called up to the pilothouse. "Captain, them Sioux want to talk, but they got war paint on!"

"I see them," the captain said. "Can you speak Sioux?"

"I can parley with my hands," he offered.

"We'll pull to shore where you can talk with them." To the pilot he said, "They're going to have to move over, but I suppose we should see what they want. Better to try and make friends than ignore them. They wouldn't like that." He stepped outside the pilothouse and ordered, "Women and children inside!"

"Come, children," Martha said, taking each by a hand and leading them through a doorway. "I'll feel better when you're safe inside."

"I would feel better if we didn't stop," Electa said, following them while looking back at James.

"We came to teach them, remember?" he said, smiling. "But for now, go to the cabins where we know it's safe."

A dozen hard-muscled, lean brown men wearing colorfully painted designs and little else waited on horses. Carter stood at the *Emilie's* bow while her paddles stopped turning. She floated silently to shore and came to a halt. Crowds of men waited on the decks. The midday heat fell down while hand and arm movements passed between them. Finally they stopped.

Still facing the Indians, Carter called out, "Captain, these worthies want to come on your boat. What do you say?"

"Come aboard? Why? We don't have time for nonsense!"

"Oh, I reckon to see what they can steal, or how many of us they can kill or count coup on."

"Tell them to stay where they are."

"They ain't goin' to like it. You'd better get moving."

The *Emilie's* paddles began to turn, slowly backing the ship up while the Indians spoke excitedly among themselves. Carter had just rejoined the crowd when arrows suddenly thumped into the ship's timber near some men.

"Everyone get down!" the captain shouted. "Swing the cannon starboard and fire when ready!"

In moments, men had the two cannons on the forward deck turned and loaded. Explosions of smoky thunder blasted from the iron mouths and echoed beyond the Indians as the shells exploded. The Sioux yelled frightful cries as they rode away through the trees and out of sight.

"Well, the man said we should be seeing Indians soon," James told Martha when it was over.

"Yes, no doubt it was certain," she replied.

The Emilie moved on upriver. Electa returned to the deck where she stopped to watch a man dig an arrow from a wall with a knife. Despite the hot day, chills moved up her back and neck. She looked away. Her thoughts wandered across the miles to the east. In a few minutes the Vails returned to the deck.

"How would we feel if we were them?" Electa said.

"Perhaps angry. They certainly are," James said.

"But we're staying on the river," Martha protested.

"While every so often we stop to cut wood for fuel," James said. "And we leave the ship to see the countryside and pick flowers, well armed in case we're attacked. Just imagine how that looks to them."

"Will we make friends with them at Sun River Farm?" Electa said, looking out across the countryside.

"Yes, with patience, I think we can," James said.

A week later, they had navigated from the Mississippi to the Missouri River, where they passed by an Indian camp that only glanced at the ship. The pilot, knowing that the tribe was peaceful, steered as close to shore as the river allowed. Curious passengers lined the railings to see what they could through the trees. The smell of the campfires floated to them in gray smoke.

"Look, by those approaching trees," Electa said. "It's a woman, kneeling. Listen, can you hear it? She's singing some sort of song."

"What is that she's under?" Martha said.

"It's a platform on posts with something on it," Electa said.

The Indian woman continued to wail while ignoring the many white faces intruding on her grief. Raising her arms, she slowly made long cuts on each one with a knife. Blood ran down her arms as she continued her haunting chant.

"Oh!" cried Electa, "what a horrible sight!" She turned away, hiding her face in Martha's shoulder. They had never imagined seeing anything like that. A deep voice behind them said, "None of us left death behind, lady. Better get used to it.

That's her husband up there on that bier. She's lettin' out her sorrow."

"She's in mourning," Electa said. "Of course, what else could it be?"

"Some take a death scene as a bad sign," the deep voice said.

Electa frowned, deciding to ignore the rude insinuation. The methodical sounds of the ship's engine and the splashing water overtook the sorrowful song as the *Emilie* continued upstream.

"Father," Electa breathed, "thank You for saving me from such a fate."

Chapter Three ~ The *Spread Eagle*

Three weeks and two thousand miles from St. Louis, the *Emilie* anchored at Fort Berthold. An oasis of civilization, the simple structure of upright logs sat by the muddy brown river in the midst of a sea of tall green grass. After breakfast, willing passengers had one hour to go ashore and stretch their legs. Surprised to see another steamship nearby, Electa approached Captain La Barge as he stood by the railing. Electa liked him. He smiled with his whole face. His mouth, showing white teeth, curved up, pushing his rosy cheeks higher and wrinkling his skin, making his eyes smile too.

"Excuse me, Captain, but where is that ship going?" she said, pointing.

"Good morning, Miss Bryan," he said, looking wistfully at the ship. "Fort Benton, I'm afraid, as we are. She's the *Spread Eagle*. She left St. Louis four days ahead of us. We've finally caught up with her, and I'll be horn-swaggled if she'll get there first." He pounded his fist on the railing in mock anger with a twinkle in his eye.

"We've been in a contest this entire time?" Electa said.

"You might say that. But it's not just a question of who gets there first. It's the freight contracts that will go to the fastest ship. Fort Benton will need many more shiploads of supplies. And, I might add, it's also a matter of honor and pride."

Muffled shouts came across the water to taunt the *Emilie* and her captain.

"There, do you see?" he said. "Pride must answer their mockery. The challenge lies clearly before us. Excuse me while we get underway." He gave her a short bow and went to the pilothouse. The ship's whistle called everyone back from shore with a wail.

Soon, the *Spread Eagle* shoved off and the *Emilie* followed, the two ships sending small waves out from their sides and black puffs of smoke behind them. Fifteen minutes later the *Emilie* passed her rival. Many passengers shouted exhilarated hurrahs at her quick victory and one might have had the feeling that the occasion was actually a light-hearted party.

But their glad spirit didn't last. Before long, the *Spread Eagle* came from behind on a new head of steam and methodically charged ahead once again. A more serious mood fell on the *Emilie*. If the water had been calm it would have reflected many concerned and serious faces. The distance between the ships slowly decreased until they eventually raced side by side. For over an hour neither was able to gain on the other. Each pilot's determination thrashed his ship's paddles furiously in the water.

"How long can this go on?" Martha asked James.

"I don't know, Dear, but I do know that our captain has the best reputation on the river, and that the Captain of our salvation will not fail us. But you ladies should take the children and go to the cabins. We've asked God to protect us, so let's not be afraid."

Martha and Electa exchanged a look, which said, "It's not easy to be calm about men's games." But they left, trusting James's judgment, knowing that he was right. Soon, a hazard in the form of an island loomed ahead, splitting the river where only one ship at a time could possibly pass. Captain La Barge stood in the pilothouse with his pilot, Ian Baker. Baker stood relaxed, at least a foot taller than the five-foot tall wheel. A blue uniform hung on his thin frame. About ten years younger than the captain, he wore long brown sideburns and a matching trim mustache. He possessed the incredibly intuitive feel for the flow of a river that his trade required.

"Captain, there's a trough of water passing portside of that island," Baker said. "The main channel makes a wide run to the starboard side, but with the river this high we're certain to be safe in the trough and faster to boot."

"Do what you must, but get us past," the captain said. Trained by years of experience, in the midst of excitement the men were as cool as the water itself, which became increasingly violent. Partially submerged boulders dotted the river around them.

"That scheming pilot of the *Spread Eagle* knows what I'm about," Baker said, "but it's almost too late for him to steer for the faster channel."

Suddenly and without warning, the *Spread Eagle*s pilot spun her wheel.

"Look out! He's going to ram us!" Captain La Barge said.

The ships collided with a terrific jolt dangerously near the *Emilie's* boilers. Women screamed, children cried, and men cursed. Everyone faced jeopardy and danger as the ships, locked together, careened out of either pilot's control.

"We're locked with the devil himself, but I wasn't born in the woods to be scared by an owl!" the captain said.

The two ships drifted as one quickly and carelessly in the strong current. Torrents of white water washed between them, splashing furiously onto the decks. Captain La Barge ordered full steam ahead. Heated threats were exchanged until the powerful river finally tore the huge ships apart. At the last possible moment, Baker angrily steered for the faster channel. When the divided river came together again, the *Emilie* had passed the *Spread Eagle* for the last time.

~

The following day, life on the ship returned to normal except for the gaping wound to the ship's deck. Incredibly beautiful white cliffs appeared on shore as the Vails sat on a blanket on the hurricane deck. Captain La Barge tipped his hat to them as he walked by.

"Good morning, Captain," James said, standing up. "We've heard rumors that we'll soon reach Fort Benton. Is that true?"

"Good morning, Mr. Vail, ladies. They're true enough. I expect we'll reach the old fort in about a week. It will take one day to unload the cargo, so your wagons and supplies won't be ready right away."

"What sort of lodging might there be at the fort for my family?"

"None fit for women and children," the captain said, shaking his head. "It's been the Indian agency for about seven years and has its share of half-breeds and wolf dogs, so I'm afraid it's not very pleasant. I wouldn't let my family stay there."

"What do you suggest?"

"Well, the safest place will be aboard until you're ready to leave."

"Thank you, that's very kind," James said, shaking his hand.

"Not at all. You've paid your fare and you're going into rough country. You'll need every favor and advantage. I hope it's not your last. Good day," he said, and went on his way.

"Well," Electa said, shaking her head, "I for one am not anxious to leave the *Emilie's* safety."

"Neither am I," Martha said, "but we've been on this ship long enough. I want to leave for Sun River Farm as soon as possible."

"As do we all," James said, sighing and patting the handrail. "But you heard him say that it's no pillow for women and children, and too dangerous for you to stay there. Besides, it really doesn't matter where we sleep."

"Well, I'm willing to sleep in a safe place," Electa said, shrugging and smiling.

"I suppose we can stand one more week on our floating castle," Martha said.

Electa looked up at the seemingly endless blue sky and a few billowing white clouds. She thought, "I have a loving family, though Mary and Harvey aren't my own. And I'm blessed with a new life on the frontier. If only my old life would stop tearing at me. I know what I need to do. I need to simply trust God to carry me in His will. Why can't I just be satisfied with what Providence has provided? Why isn't life more simple? I know that God will bring the answers in His own time, but perhaps He won't make me wait very long."

Chapter Four ~ The Mullan Road

One week later, the *Emilie* finally came in sight of Fort Benton. The July heat had turned the riverside hills brown, which added to the desolate appearance of the fort. Mostly made of adobe brick, the only log building was a barn. Faded American flags flew atop two guard towers on opposing corners. The Vail family waited as patiently as possible with everyone else for the ship to dock and let down her wide gangplank.

"This is so exciting!" Electa said, as she, Martha, and the children watched most of the *Emilie's* human cargo deposited slowly onto the shore and then into the fort.

"I'm afraid for my babies," Martha said, stroking Harvey's hair.

"I'm sure we'll all be fine," Electa said, placing an arm around her shoulder.

Within Fort Benton, James walked into the general store for supplies. Small barrels of whiskey, beer, ginger beer, and vinegar sat on rough-hewn boards. Shelves hung on the walls, holding clothing, candles, oil lamps, tins of salt, sugar, spices, and dozens of other items needed by the gold camps. Dust floated in stifled sunlight as it struggled to shine through parchment windows. But nothing could cut the stench of whiskey, cigar smoke, and filthy men. James sighed, thankful that his family remained on the *Emilie*, and went to the rear of the store to place his order. He held out the list to a clerk in a canvas apron standing behind a counter of sorts, and asked, "Friend, can you tell me how the Mullan Road is?"

Suddenly a heavy red-faced man clenching a cigar in a yellow-toothed grin put a hand on James's shoulder, took the list from the clerk and said, "That dugway will shake your boots off. Just as rough as a cob." His yellow smile faded. "And no one here is your friend," he said, crumpling the paper. James frowned and reached to retrieve it in vain as the man stopped him. Men at a corner table laughed.

"Here now, what do you think you're doing?" James demanded.

In the next instant a pistol barrel pointed between James's eyes.

"I don't think," the man said, "I know. And you'd better know who can do what in this place. I can do anything I please, and you'll do what I say."

"On second thought, you'd better think again," Francis said from behind the man, his own pistol at the man's side. "Give the paper back."

The tough gave his golden grin and sighed. "I was just seein' what I could get away with. No harm done. Here, storekeep', fetch the pilgrim's stuff," he said, dropping his gun on the floor and handing him the paper. The storekeeper disgustedly took it.

"No harm done to you and that's what counts, now, isn't it?" James said, backing away, and taking out his own pistol.

"Sure, and that's the way of it, but what d'ya suppose could happen on the trail?"

"Nothing, if you would like to remain as healthy, wealthy, and wise as you seem to think you are," Francis said.

"Benjamin Franklin. Very good," James said, smiling.

"Thank you," Francis replied, still gazing at the man. "Let me assure you, sir, that we'll keep more than one eye open for road thieves and white rubbish."

The tough's face turned crimson as Francis and James backed up past open barrels of apples, crackers, pickles, and stacked sacks of flour and coffee beans.

"This much will take two men all day to gather up," the storekeeper said, waving James's list as though it was an inconvenience, and not his business.

"We'll be back. Just make sure it's all there when we come for it," James said.

"Pilgrims, you might do all right," the clerk said. Looking at the red-faced tough he added, "But keep an eye open as you said or you'll be up to the hub."

"Thank you, but our men will be ready for any trouble."

"How many in your party?" asked the tough.

"Enough to get my family safely to our farm," James said.

"Farm?" the man laughed. "You're a farmer? Most pilgrims this far west farm gold. What're you gonna farm?"

The men sitting at the tables laughed. James and Francis nodded at one another and left through the door. When they reached the fort's gate they saw roustabouts unloading the *Emilie*. At the water's edge they found Captain La Barge, who, as they approached, pointed at buckboard wagons being pulled off the ship's platforms.

"There are your wagons, gentlemen. The horses are all sound and strong. I hope you arrive safely at your destination with Godspeed. I wish all my passengers would be as pleasant to have aboard as you have been. Goodbye."

"Thank you and goodbye," James said. They shook hands and the captain went to board the *Emilie*.

As they watched the unloading, James said, "Thank you for driving my other team, Francis. Otherwise, Martha would have to."

"I'm just glad we both have friends to travel with," Francis replied, grinning.

James's family greeted them from the hurricane deck and the men waved back. Francis sighed and said, "Electa will make some man a wonderful wife, but she and I don't quite fit. Her passions are both the old life she left behind and her new life here, a paradox I cannot understand."

James patted him on the back. "Give her time," he said. "You haven't known her very long. Granted, she is a mystery, one that no man has yet solved. You'll get to know her better while riding together. Then, if you feel you want to offer her your heart, maybe she'll take it, and give you hers in return," he said, only half teasing.

"Don't count on anything like that," Francis replied.

"Well," James said, "we'll see. Whatever happens, I want you to know that your acquaintance has come to mean quite a lot to my family. Especially to me. The farther west we go, the fewer men there are that can be trusted."

"Much obliged; I feel the same way about you folks. I'll help you and yours all I can," Francis said.

"Tell your men to have their guns at the ready," James said, and the men shook hands before boarding the ship and going to their cabins for the night.

~

The next morning after breakfast, James escorted his family from the *Emilie* to their wagons and announced, "All right, ladies, it's time to climb up now; we're ready to go." Everything they would need had been packed, covered with canvas tarps, and tied down.

"You're sure everything is secure?" Martha said, frowning. She placed an arm around Mary and Harvey who sat beside her.

"It's been over a month since I've hitched horses to a wagon and tied knots in rope, but I think I can remember how," he teased. "Four wagons with four horses each will do the job. Francis and his men will leave us at the farm, and when the time comes I'll come back for more supplies."

"James, alone?" Martha asked.

"Unless I can find some help, which I doubt, since everyone in sight has gold fever. Don't worry, you'll know how to shoot a rifle by then."

He slapped the reins on the horse's backs, clucking his tongue. The other wagons slowly followed them through the gate. James turned to look behind, where Electa sat next to Francis. Martha noticed.

"And why did you have Electa ride in Mr. Thompson's wagon?" she teased.

"And where else was she going to ride, I'd like to know? Besides, they do make a nice-looking couple."

"Perhaps, but Francis needs a fancier lady than Electa," Martha said.

"Maybe so, maybe no."

As the wagons climbed the western bluff leaving the river valley, Martha said, "James, do you think we'll be safe?"

"Do you mean on this trip, on the farm, or both?"

"I mean until we get there."

"We're well armed. We'll be all right," he said, grinning reassuringly.

"There are no guarantees out here, are there James?"

"None but the Lord's, my dear."

She contentedly slipped her arm through his. Behind them, Electa arranged her seat blanket as a cushion.

"How I miss our Dearborn," she sighed.

"Yes, but your one-horse Dearborn would never carry what these buckboard wagons can. I wonder if you will ever see a Dearborn in Idaho Territory," Francis said.

"If I do it will only serve to remind me of home."

"Electa, this place, all of it," he said, making a great sweeping gesture, "this is your home now, and the sooner you consider it to be so, the happier you'll be."

He wondered how she would take his unasked-for advice, but thought he had known her long enough to take the liberty.

"But how does one do that?" she said. "Can I, in one moment, erase an entire lifetime of memories? Of home, and family, and friends, and instantly make a new life here? No, I'm afraid it will take much longer than I care to think about."

"But what if you found someone you cared for, someone who could take your mind off the past?" he asked.

"Well, if that man is alive I would certainly like to meet him," she said, and they laughed. She thought, "Who and what might such a man be?"

"I can't imagine marrying a miner," she said, "or a man who has lived in these mountains for years, and what sort does that leave?"

"Well, maybe you'll meet someone sooner than you think."

"I realize," she said with a deep sigh, "that I accepted all of this before leaving Ohio and coming so far, and that now I have to face life here. So, I hereby resolve to look ahead." Pursing her lips and crossing her arms in a determined sort of way, she announced, "Self pity is not a practice I am used to and it is certainly not a Christian virtue. My heart aches, but I know that I must leave my past where it is and must be. I can't go there except in my memories, which I do admit are some comfort, but I can't live there every day."

If she was to survive the mountain wilderness, even thrive in it and learn to conquer it, she must live in the present and look ahead. The bumpy Mullan Road led to her future.

"Why is it," she said, "that both anticipation and dread make time seem to pass more slowly than it really does?"

Francis glanced at her with raised eyebrows. "Well," he said, "for someone waiting for time to pass, if it seems to slow down, then perhaps it really does. Would that be you?"

"How could you tell?" she laughed. "Now that I have resolved to let the past go, I must admit that I am excited! Tomorrow we'll reach the farm, and Martha and I will clean the house and set everything just the way she wants it."

"I'm glad you're not fairly dreading this place any longer. One resolution does not a life make, but it is a grand beginning for a grand place."

She sat up straight, holding onto her seat to smooth the bumps, and frowned at him.

"I'll have you know, Mr. Thompson, that I am a woman of resolve, and when I put my mind to something, I do it. Of course I miss my home. Who wouldn't? But I'm here now. I'm going to accept whatever God has for me and make the most of this place."

She had wanted to say "whoever" but thought better of it. A man wouldn't understand. He would just laugh and tease her, and later tell James, and together they would make fun of her romantic dreams.

James looked at his pocket watch. "Let's stop here. It's time to eat," he said, holding an arm up to signal the wagons.

"The captain gave us this fried chicken for our trip," Martha said. "He is such a nice man."

She also gave everyone a can of sweet peaches, offered cold cider, and made a large pot of hot coffee. The fresh mountain air seemed to make the meal even more delicious. An hour later, the wagons again stirred up brown dust while creaking down the Mullan Road. That evening, the sun shot long pink streaks across the sky and the air turned refreshingly cool.

"It will be dark soon," James said. "We should stop for the night along this stream. We've gone far enough for the day, I suppose."

The women climbed down with some help, and laughed when they saw each other stretching.

"Have you ever been so stiff and sore?" Electa said.

"No, and I know you haven't, either," Martha laughed. James put an arm around her and kissed her cheek.

"It shouldn't take long for the men to bring in some fresh meat," he said. "Francis and I will take care of the horses."

Before long, one of the men arrived with a deer thrown over a horse. Pie and johnnycake cooked in a Dutch oven while skewered roasts hung over the fire. After supper the women finished washing pans and dishes. Electa saw a man retrieve a small accordion from a wagon.

"Oh, no, now the men will want to dance. I'm so tired I don't think I can," she groaned, packing pans in a wagon.

"Martha, come dance around the fire," James called, and the man began to play.

"They have strength enough because they didn't wash the dishes," Martha said, only half joking.

Francis approached Electa as she finished packing. "May I have the pleasure of this dance?" he asked.

"Oh, I suppose, but only because I'm too stubborn to admit how tired I am."

After going around and around to "My Old Aunt Sally" and "Sweet Betsy from Pike," the women excused themselves, said good night, and the men thanked them. Crawling under the wagons, they wrapped themselves in blankets beside the children. Morning air of the second day was cool and fresh. Light dew washed the grass. Breakfast was done about the time summer heat warmed the air and dried the grass. The Vail family climbed into their wagons with light hearts and good spirits. The road was no smoother, but for them it was shorter. Francis's crew would continue west. Before very long the sun was high and they stopped to rest and eat the noon meal. Afterward the ladies packed things away while the men smoked and the children played. James walked alone to the crest of the nearest hill.

"Look!" he said, pointing. "It's the Sun River! From here we just follow it to the farm!"

Electa and Martha hurriedly picked up the children to see, and the men followed. Standing in awe, they admired the beautiful valley scene. The wet ribbon called Sun River wandered west, leading the way to their new home.

"The sky seems as big as heaven itself," Electa said. James clapped his hands in excited joy.

"Let's get going," he said, laughing.

The last few hours seemed like an entire day, but before sundown several log buildings surrounded by a stake fence came into view. Sun River Farm sat between a low plateau and the river, where a ferry made of logs waited to follow a rope across to the other side.

"Here we are," James announced.

"Praise God," Martha said, hugging Mary and Harvey.

The creaking wagons stopped inside the compound. Electa stood up to search the landscape before stepping down. To the north and south she saw green grassland rising up to hills that became flat benches dotted with deer, elk, and antelope.

"So this is Sun River Farm," she said quietly. "It's paradise." She closed her eyes to pray silently. "Lord God, You know my heart and what is best for me. I leave my future to You. I only ask that if you've planned a husband for me that I love him more than life. Thank You for the men who helped us to reach this beautiful place."

"Welcome to your new home," Francis said, interrupting her thoughts. "Here, let me help you down."

"Thank you," she said, stepping down from the wagon. "I was afraid it wouldn't seem like home, and I can't explain it, but somehow it does."

Looking at her family he said, "I think I know why. Home is where the heart is, not to mention family."

She placed her arm through his and they went inside the log house to see her new home.

~

James had promised to situate their small stove the very first day, so the next morning the women cooked breakfast over a fire for the last time. The men unpacked the Vail wagons and carried everything inside. An outbuilding stood away from the main house, a smaller cabin where hired men would sleep. While Martha organized her kitchen, Electa packed a lunch for Francis and his men. They insisted on leaving right away, so they hitched their teams and got ready. James stood before them with his thumbs cocked in his suspenders and sleeves rolled up.

"Men, thank you for helping us," he said. "May God bless and watch over you."

"And the same to you," Francis said, slapping him on the back and smiling. He quietly added, "Remember what I said about Indians." He turned to Martha and Electa with hat in hand, bowed, and said, "Ladies, thank you for such wonderful repasts."

"You are quite welcome, Francis," Martha said, grinning. "You and your men stop on your way back if you can."

Taking Electa's hand he kissed it and said, "Enjoy your new life."

"Thank you, I will," she said, smiling.

"Until next time, friends," he said, climbing into his seat.

They waved goodbye as reins slapped on horse's backs and the wagons rolled to the gate. James walked to the river to work the ferry for them, which held only one wagon at a time. When they were all across, he waved goodbye again. As he turned toward the compound, he saw mounted Indians watching from the plateau several hundreds yards away.

Chapter Five ~ Joseph Swift

By late September James had discovered that the Blackfeet Indians weren't nearly as disposed to farming as he had hoped. They kept a threatening yet distant presence. James had only one opportunity to explain to them why his family had come, and even then none of the Indians would dismount, refusing to even consider breaking the skin of the land. The apparent leader listened angrily, raised his hand, and cut the air with a sharp knifelike action. That was the last time they had come to the farm.

Late September also found nineteen-year-old Philadelphian Joseph Swift at the Fort Benton general store. He had a youthful, friendly round face and wore clean clothes. A floppy brown hat topped his matching hair and eyes.

"What are you lookin' for, pilgrim?" asked the apron-clad storekeeper.

"Work. How far to the government farm on Sun River?"

"Sixty miles west on the Mullan Road. You a miner? You'll need supplies."

"No, I won't. When did the Vails come through?"

"The farmer what took it over come through here about midsummer."

"I'll be thankin' you," Joseph said, and paid for his supplies. Next, he found the blacksmith where he bought two horses: a stout bay mare to ride and a packer. That night, ten miles later down the Mullan Road, Joseph camped in a draw by a rippling stream under a clear evening sky. Surrounded by yellow cottonwood leaves, he sat on a red blanket and roasted a rabbit over his fire. In a cool breeze the creaking, groaning trees sounded like rusty door hinges begging for grease.

Suddenly, an Indian stepped from the darkness wearing fringed pants and a U.S. Army blue woolen shirt. Joseph noticed firelight reflecting from both a rifle and a knife. His heart beat faster as his stomach fluttered.

"If that don't set a body back," he thought. "Wonder if he's alone."

"What do you want? I mean no harm," Joseph said, not moving. The Indian placed a hand on his stomach while pointing his rifle at the fire.

"Want to eat?" Joseph asked. "Come on in. Sorry I called you late to supper."

The man approached, squatted, pulled out his knife, cut off a piece, and ate. Joseph did the same. They ate silently while watching one another. Apparently finished, the Indian wiped his greasy hands on his shirt and said, "Name Iron."

Joseph held out his hand. "Joseph," he offered, and the brown hand accepted his friendship. The somber man got up and returned to the darkness as quiet as a cat. Relief washed over Joseph, relaxing him. Rifle in hand, he lay down and was soon asleep.

~

Two days later he had reached Sun River Farm by late afternoon. "Hello the house!" he called out. James, repairing a harness in the barn, picked up his rifle and went to the door.

"Who is it and what do you want?" he called back.

"Joseph Swift from St. Louis. I heard you might need help."

"Are you alone?"

"I am that."

James carried his rifle to the fence and opened the gate. He saw Joseph sitting on the bay holding the rope to a packhorse and asked, "Why come this far for farm work?"

"Ma died of consumption and Pa was killed at Shiloh. I'm no coward but it's not my war. I left to make a new start. Why is that Indian tent inside your fence?"

"James Vail," James said, and held out his hand.

"Joseph Swift, sir," he said, shaking James's hand. "Pleased to meet you."

"The Piegans think they have property rights to everything in sight. The one that belongs to that tent said his tribe gets upset when we kill buffalo, so I hired him to provide our meat. We're here to get along with them and teach them, not to cause trouble. He's not hostile, keeps his distance, and does his job. As far as the war goes, you'll find that it got here before you did."

"His name Iron?" Joseph said.

"You must have met."

"In a way. He didn't keep as much distance from my supper as I would have liked."

James laughed. "Indians get as hungry as anyone else. The Piegans are part of the Blackfoot tribe if that means anything to you. Since you're a farmer and came all this way, you must know how to do an honest day's work."

"I do that. Worked my way on the *Spread Eagle* and heard no complaints."

"Oh, yes, the ship that rammed us on the river. I have often wondered if that pilot was horsewhipped."

"That was a while back," Joseph said, "but I heard tell his men had to guard the ship while at Fort Benton after that."

"Vengeance is the Lord's. I have no hard feelings toward the man," James said, leaning on his gun. He frowned thoughtfully. "Tell me, are you a God-fearing man?"

"I go to church when I can, but I don't see one around here," he said, looking.

"True enough. I thought as much, from the looks of you. There may not be a church here but we do keep the Christian Sabbath. That means that there is no work done for me on that day. We also need a man who can shoot straight. Can you hit that knot of wood?" James said, pointing at a tree stump some distance away.

Joseph stepped down off his horse, pulled his pistol from its holster, aimed, and fired. At the sound of the blast, wood flew from where the knot had been. They both grinned. If they had looked at the house they would have seen Electa and Martha peering out the window.

"What is he shooting about?" Electa said, wiping her dishwater-wet hands on her apron. Martha stood at the table kneading dough. "I hope that's an answer to our prayers," she said. "I'm sure James is talking to him about staying on."

"He's not a bad-looking young man from what I can see," Electa said.

"You're not setting store by looks alone, are you dear?" Martha teased. "You know the Lord doesn't want us to do that."

"Well, one has to start somewhere and from here I can't tell what his heart is like," Electa teased back. Outside, James made an offer to Joseph.

"Well, young Joseph, what do you think? Want to give it a try?"

"Yes, sir," Joseph said, smiling.

"Good. Get settled in that cabin over there," James said, pointing at the small building behind the house, "and you can start work in the morning."

"Thank you, Mr. Vail," Joseph said.

Outside the cabin a washbasin sat on a stump with a bucket beside it. A lone parchment window faced east where it could receive daybreak sun. Inside, two pine pole bunks furnished both the north and south walls. A small woodstove stood in the middle of the back on the dirt floor. Joseph washed his face and tossed his bedroll on a bottom bunk. A bell rang at the main house and he met James at the cabin's door.

"Supper is ready. Are you?" James said.

"I'm always ready to eat," Joseph replied, grinning.

The aromas of sourdough bread, beans, coffee, chipped beef, and gravy met them as they entered the small one story log house. Mary and Harvey stopped playing and stared at Joseph. Martha and Electa worked by tallow lamps and candlelight since the house, too, had but one parchment window. The main room served as kitchen, dining room, and parlor. Two doors led to back bedrooms. Electa shared one with the children, and James and Martha slept in the other. Rugs covered the hard-packed dirt floor. Cloth covered several walls, which helped brighten the dark rooms. A likeness of President Lincoln hung honorably in the main room.

"Ladies, I would like you to meet the newest resident of Sun River Farm, Mr. Joseph Swift. Joseph, I'd like you to meet my wife, Mrs. Martha Vail, our children, Mary and Harvey, and my sister-in-law, Miss Electa Bryan."

"Nice to make your acquaintance," he said.

"You're most welcome here, Joseph," Martha said, smiling. "I'm glad James finally has some help."

"Pleased to meet you, Miss," he said to Electa.

"Hello, Mr. Swift."

"Please, just call me Joseph. And hello to you two," he said to the children. Mary smoothed her dress and smiled shyly. Harvey bit his lip and shuffled his bare feet.

"How long since you've had a hot meal, Joseph?" Martha asked.

"Not since the ship, ma'am. It sure smells good."

"Please sit down. You can't go to bed hungry."

"Let's thank God," James said after they were all situated. "Heavenly Father, our hearts are grateful for this food. Bless the hands that labored to prepare it. Thank You for bringing Joseph here safely. In the Name of Jesus Christ our Lord, amen." Looking at Joseph, James said, "What's happening at the fort, Joseph? We haven't heard any news for days now."

"Well, sir, the Indians attacked mackinaws on the river, so the boatmen won't float passengers until things settle down. Quite a few folks are waiting, but no steamships are coming before spring."

"The Lord has brought you at a good time, but we still need more protection and help to prepare for winter. In the morning

I'll take a wagon to Fort Benton for supplies and try to hire another man or two. I won't be gone a week."

After dinner, Joseph warned his new boss when they were alone outside.

"Mr. Vail, I didn't want to say anything at dinner, but you'd best keep a rifle in hand the whole way. I only saw Iron on the way here but that doesn't mean there aren't hostiles about."

"I know. I haven't said anything to the women, but Blackfeet have been watching us for weeks. Two men I ferried across the river last week told me rumors of miners being killed and I half believe it. I don't want to go, but if I can find more men at Fort Benton we'll all feel safer."

"Yes, sir, I know I would."

The following morning, James told Joseph about Francis Thompson while they walked to the shed. There, an odd-shaped form sat covered with heavy brown tarp. "Let me show you what our good friend Francis left behind for us," James said, lifting one end of the tarp. Joseph's eyes grew wide.

"A cannon!" Joseph said.

"What do you think? He thought we might need it and could better protect ourselves."

"I should say so. It's not very big though, is it?"

"She's big enough to put the fear of God into anyone who attacks us. I don't embrace violence, but I've learned that there are times when a man must protect his family. Even against those he would rather help."

"You mean Indians."

"It's turned out that they might be more inclined to fighting than farming. Just roll her outside, pick up the tail, and swing it around to aim. Here, I'll show you how to load her," he said, patting the cannon. "Scoop two handfuls of gunpowder out of that barrel and pour them down the mouth. Roll one of these twelve-pound balls down and pack it tight with this rod. Point her in the right direction, set a torch to this hole, and she'll belch hellfire."

"How far will it reach?"

"About a hundred yards or so. You'll just have to throw a few balls their way and hope for the best. We haven't had any trouble yet, and I trust you won't before I return. Be sure to carry your gun when you go to the river." Joseph nodded his understanding.

James packed food, a rifle, ropes, and tarps to secure the new supplies. After kissing Martha and hugging Mary and Harvey, he shook Joseph's hand. A knowing look passed between them. "Strange," he thought, "how such trust can run between men in a short time."

"Don't forget the sugar and tea," Martha said.

"If they have it," he promised, smiling.

"Would you post these letters for us?" Electa asked.

"Of course," he said, tucking them into his pocket. He climbed into the wagon and left his family in Joseph's hands.

Electa had written Victoria.

Dear Victoria;   September 28, 1862

I hope you are well. We are fine but isolated. The beauty of this place does not help with loneliness, and I miss everyone terribly. Last night James hired Mr. Joseph Swift but there is much work to be done before winter and we are still short-handed. James has gone to Fort Benton in an attempt to hire more men. He has cultivated a number of acres but cannot interest the Indians in farming. They are clean but stubborn and fearsome. Pray that he won't be discouraged.

I enjoy helping with the children. Martha and I have turned the cabin into a fine, comfortable home. We must use sugar and tea sparingly and then only on special occasions. Mr. Swift is a fine young Christian man but my Prince Charming has not yet arrived. It would be a great miracle if he were to do so in this far-flung place, but I know God has a reason for my being here. He is with us and we trust in Him. We are many miles from the nearest gold camps and settlements. Pray for us.

Yours devotedly, Electa Bryan

Chapter Six ~ Your Servant, Henry Plummer

James saw no one on the Mullan Road. When he reached the fort he saw a good many people camped in tents. Some had even built log houses, which surprised him.

"There must be men here who need work," he thought.

Much more freight sat stacked near the river than before. He spoke to two men near the gate who stood leaning against the adobe fort's wall.

"Hello you gents. Might you be needing work?"

One of them, less than clean and looking less than friendly, had a black, scruffy beard. He stopped whittling on the stick he'd been working on long enough to look up from under his hat, but didn't say anything. The other one wore a clean dark suit coat, striped pants, white shirt, bow tie, and a smile. He answered James.

"Well, I was heading to the States but can't do that just yet. Not sure I want to anyway. What have you got?" he said.

"I run a government farm sixty miles west. It's not a gold mine, but there's honest work, a cabin, and home cooking. I already have one good man, but need two more before winter sets in. Interested?"

The two men looked at each other. The unshaven one shrugged.

"We'd like a time to think it over, but I will shake your hand. The name is Henry Plummer."

"How do you do, Mr. Plummer," James said, reaching down to shake his hand.

"This here is Jack Cleveland," Plummer said, nodding his head at the man.

"Hello, Mr. Cleveland," James said.

"Jack will do," the man said, remaining against the wall. "What about Indians? You having trouble?" Jack asked.

"That's part of it. Can you shoot?" James said.

"Mister, I make a fist at whatever I aim at," Jack said, standing up straight and facing James.

"No offense intended, but I had to ask," James said, smiling. "You understand."

"He's right, Jack. Mr. Vail, we don't kick at hard work and you'll find us well qualified when trouble comes," Henry said.

"Good. If you sign on, we'll have four men, and I don't think we'll be bothered very much. I'll buy my supplies now. Let me know when I get back. Fair enough?"

"Fair enough," Henry said.

James drove his wagon inside the fort while Jack continued to whittle.

"What do you think?" Jack said. He wore a constant frown over nervous, jumpy eyes. His dirty, dark hair, shoved straight back, hung over his collar. They made an odd pair; Jack was rough, plain looking, and impatient, while Henry was clean, polite, good-looking, and soft-spoken. Maybe each balanced the other out.

"Reckon we can't stay here," Henry said. "There's no going east and I need a stake before heading back to the diggings. Sounds like a pretty good way to winter."

"Anything is better than just sitting here," Jack said. "I'll get the horses."

Men with only a packhorse could be ready to travel quickly. James returned two hours later with his wagon loaded, ready to go.

"You men need to understand a few things before you decide to come with me. All card playing and whiskey will be kept inside the cabin and there will be no cursing within hearing distance of my family. We're God-fearing people and I won't stand for it. Are you working for me or should I keep looking?"

They looked at each other. Jack tipped his hat back, raised his eyebrows, and looked at James.

"We are if the offer still stands," Henry said, smiling. Jack only nodded.

"Traveling together will be safer for us all. Are you ready?"

"Ready and waiting, Mr. Vail," Henry said, and they mounted their horses.

"Good. I expect we'll get along just fine."

They made fifteen miles before sunset. After a supper of beans, biscuits, and coffee, Henry and Jack played cards by firelight.

"Play a hand, Mr. Vail?" Jack said.

"No, thank you. I think better of God's supply than to gamble. What you do is your business," James said.

"Did I tell you about the two gentlemen me and Charlie Reeves camped with near Cottonwood?" Henry said.

Jack merely grunted and frowned as he fingered his cards. James didn't think Henry was talking to him.

"Called themselves the Stuart brothers, Granville and James. They talked Charlie and me into going up to Hell Gate with them and back to Gold Creek. We went with them because they were card players. If I didn't need the work I wouldn't have come with you," Henry said, grinning at James.

"We're all here for a reason," James said.

"I'm here to play cards," Jack said. "Are you going to play or jabber?"

"The first night I won the pot and they fixed my shotgun besides," Henry said. "Gold Creek didn't hold much promise so we rode on to the Beaverhead mines."

"Is mining how you usually make your living?" James said.

"Gold or silver, makes no difference to me," Henry said.

"That and wearing a badge," Jack said. He raised one eyebrow and gave Henry a hard look.

"Jack can't abide most lawmen," Henry said, "but he puts up with me for some reason."

"I'm as law-abiding as the next man," Jack said.

"I'm glad to hear that," James said.

"Depends on the next man," Henry teased, which Jack scowled at. They were up and on the trail early. James hurried along since he wanted to get back as soon as possible. They arrived at Sun River Farm two days later just before dark, tired but safe. Joseph saw them coming and opened the gate.

"Hello, Mr. Vail, glad to see you. I see that you got what you went after. Any Indian trouble?" he said.

"Hello, Joseph. Not one bit," James said as he rode by.

"Howdy," Joseph said to the men. Jack just nodded. Henry tipped his hat and grinned. "You must be Joseph," he said, leaning over to shake his hand.

"Henry Plummer, and that's Jack Cleveland. He's not very chirpy after riding all day."

"That's all right. Getting tired myself from cutting wood all day."

"That'll do it," Henry said with a smile, and nudged his horse.

Martha and Electa came out of the house. Henry and Jack exchanged glances when they saw them. Martha smiled but waited until they reached the house before saying anything.

"You weren't gone a week and brought two men back! The Lord is watching over us," she said, hugging James.

"I have no doubt of that, but I'm afraid there was no sugar, tea, or salt at Fort Benton, though I did post your letters. There are more people than supplies there. We'll just have to make do. Allow me to introduce these gentlemen. Mr. Jack Cleveland, my wife, Mrs. Martha Vail, and my sister-in-law, Miss Electa Bryan."

Jack stayed mounted while tipping his hat. "Ladies," he said.

"And this is Mr. Henry Plummer."

Henry dismounted and removed his hat as he approached Martha. "Pleased to meet you, ma'am," he said, smiling.

They shook hands and he gave a slight bow. As he turned to Electa, she held out her hand. He took it, locked in a gaze with her, bowed, and gently kissed it. She blushed. James and Martha looked at one another with raised eyebrows.

"Your servant, Henry Plummer," he said.

Chapter Seven ~ A New Friend

Dear Victoria,   October 1, 1862

James brought your letter of August. I am thankful for your good health, but of course was saddened to hear of your father's death in the war. I know that his faith in Christ is a great comfort to you. We are all well. I am eager to tell you of a most exciting man named Henry Plummer. He is one of two more men which James hired from Fort Benton. Mr. Plummer is quite the gentleman. I do not know him very well yet, but from conversation at dinner last night he seems to be intelligent, well-mannered, and very clean. The other man, Mr. Jack Cleveland, is nice enough but is sorely lacking in table manners and cleanliness. Henry asked if he could escort me on a walk tomorrow evening, when, he said, "You can tell me about yourself, and we can get to know one another better." He has a distinct northeastern accent since he is from Maine. He is four or five inches taller than me, of medium build, and is soft spoken. I wonder if he is my "Knight in Shining Armor," but must determine whether he is a believer or not. Of less importance, but of no less interest, is his appearance. Virginia, he is handsome and a very polished man. The color of his eyes seems to wander between gray and blue. His hair is a wavy light brown that hints with red, at least in candlelight. I will not end this letter until I tell you of our walk tomorrow night.

~

The next day, Henry talked to James about Electa. "Mr. Vail, could I have a word with you about Miss Electa?"

"Of course. What about her?" James said, grinning.

The four men had worked all day repairing the fence surrounding the compound. James wanted it too high for horses to jump and high enough for a man to stand behind and shoot over if necessary.

"Well, sir, I asked her to walk with me this evening without first gaining your permission. I apologize."

"I see," James said, picking up some nails. "That's all right. I recall asking Martha's father if we could court." A remembering look in his eyes distanced him from the moment. He paused, grinning as though he understood. "The county we came from had better prospects than me, but it seems she had already picked me out from the herd. But, I'm not Electa's father so this isn't quite the same thing. I'm willing as long as she is. Just stay in the compound. We have to be careful with the Indians."

"Yes, sir. And, my intentions are honorable, I assure you. My mother taught me to respect women."

"I'm glad to hear it. Electa is a fine woman. Loyal to her family to a fault, if that's possible. She hasn't been ready for a man up to now, but I believe coming out here has made her quite ready."

Embarrassed, Henry played in yellow cottonwood leaves with the toe of his boot. He breathed in deeply. "Sure smells like winter is coming," he said. The sky hung heavy in gray, yet the clouds were high enough that new snow could be seen on the mountains.

"You must know that she has been of marrying age for some time," James said. "She has her own mind and a strong will which you should look out for. I only ask that you treat her as well as she deserves. You'll find her a challenge, but she's honest and will expect the same from you. Her heart is her own business, but I warn you. Hurt any other part of her and you'll answer to me."

"Yes, sir. I assure you that I have the highest regard for her. I expect Jack to ask her to go on a walk too. I don't know him real well, so he'll have to stand on his own. We've worked and traveled some together, but we're not best friends."

"Don't let her see the two of you fall out and fight over her. There's nothing worse than a puffed up female," James said with a grin.

"No, sir, I expect so."

They laughed together, and Henry excused himself. They had enough time before dinner to wash up. Henry had carried water from the river several times during the day, so he had a little time with Electa then. In her nervous words and stolen glances, he took hope that she was anxious as well. That evening, he complimented the women.

"Ladies, that was a fine dinner. When we come in, every meal smells like heaven, looks just grand, and nothing can outdo the taste."

"Thank you," Martha said smiling, looking at Electa. "We're glad you men are here to enjoy it. Electa and I are used to cooking for a lot of people."

"Yes, we are," Electa said as she gathered dishes.

"Miss Electa?" Henry said, standing up from the table.

"Yes, Mr. Plummer?"

"If it's all right, I'll call on you when you're done helping Mrs. Vail."

She blushed as everyone except Jack smiled.

"Yes, that would be fine," she replied. "I won't be very long."

"She'll be out by and by, Henry," Martha said.

"Yes, ma'am, thank you."

He excused himself and got up to leave. Walking to the hat rack he noticed Jack staring at the table, more somber than usual. Joseph saw it too and said, "Excuse me, I've got chores."

After they left, Jack's eyebrows raised with expectation and hope, but he continued to look at the table as he spoke nervously.

"Miss Electa?"

"Yes, Mr. Cleveland?" she said, pouring hot dishwater.

"Miss Electa, would you walk with me sometime?"

With wide pleading eyes, she looked at Martha, who was also surprised. James cleared his throat to get their attention. Looking first at Jack, he winked at each lady and slightly nodded his head to Electa.

"Why, of course," she said. "I couldn't rightly go with Henry and not with you. I'll be glad to look forward to it," she said.

Jack's expression brightened considerably as he stood up and faced her.

"You just let me know when. Anytime is fine with me," he said, now excited. He excused himself as the other men had and got his hat from the rack.

"Oh, how about tomorrow evening?" she said, wiping a dish. "We need to enjoy this nice fall weather while we can. Winter is coming, you know."

"Yes, ma'am, I know. I'll be thankin' you," he said, and left.

As soon as the door shut, James and Martha quietly laughed. Electa smiled, but was too embarrassed and proud to join them.

"I believe we have a belle on our hands," James said.

"Oh, James, they're just lonely," Electa said. "When they move on they'll forget all about me." But she hoped that wasn't true concerning Henry.

"I doubt that," Martha said. "The Lord works in mysterious ways, even here. But you'd better walk softly. We don't know these men. And they have guns."

"Now, dear, they have to have guns," James said, picking up Mary and Harvey. "I do, too. No one is safe without one with the Indians out of sorts. Better to have one than to get yourself killed. I thought when we came here that just because I was a peaceful man, the Indians would be the same way. Unfortunately, that's not so."

"Well, I suppose guns are a necessary evil," Martha said, "but I don't like those two competing for you in such close quarters. You take care, young lady. Henry is handsome, but you don't yet know what he's like on the inside."

"Yes, Mother," Electa teased.

"Well, that's all I'm going to say. Just don't come to me complaining about a broken heart."

Electa and James exchanged grins. She put the last of the dishes away and said, "I'm going to get ready for my walk with Henry now." Shutting the door to her room she prayed silently, thanking God for new companionship.

Martha sat down at the table and said, "James, what if she becomes serious about one of these men?"

"What if she does?" he said.

"He may take her away to some mining camp or back east where we might never see her again."

"Yes, that might happen, but don't you think you're jumping ahead just a little? She hasn't even gone on a walk with either one of them yet."

"No, but she's about to, and then what?"

"Then, I expect the Lord will watch over her just as He's always done. And I expect we should let her live her own life, as she should, which won't be easy for either one of you." Martha smiled and sighed in resignation. She got up to look out the window, saw Henry waiting, and went to Electa's door.

"Someone outside is waiting for someone in here," she teased.

"I'm coming," Electa called through the door. "Very amusing," she said as she emerged, tossing her best shawl around her shoulders. "I suppose you'll be watching us the whole time."

"No, but we would if we could," James teased.

She waited at the door several moments for Henry to knock, which he finally did. But before she opened it, she stuck her tongue out at James, and laughed for getting in the last tease before leaving.

Chapter Eight ~ The Walk

"Hello, Miss Electa," Henry said, his hat in hand.

"Hello, Mr. Plummer," she replied and shut the door behind her.

He held out his hand to suggest the direction in which they might go. They began to stroll at a slow, comfortable pace under a golden canopy of evening sky as sunbeams glanced off billowing clouds above them.

"You look real nice," he said.

"Thank you."

"Tell me about yourself," he said.

"You already know half of what there is. What would you like to know?"

"All you'll tell me."

She laughed. Her heart beat faster with an excitement she had never felt before. At the gate they began to make their way around the perimeter of the compound, which was as far as they could go from the cabin. A cool fall breeze stirred the cottonwoods, loosing yellow leaves, which floated down around them.

"Well, I'm used to being around a lot of people," she said. "Friends at church, the children I taught in school and their parents, and neighbors. I know James is bothered about the Indians not wanting to learn how to farm, but I've had a very lonely time. I don't think he knows how isolated I've felt."

Henry looked around and chuckled. "Yes, we are that," he said. "Fort Benton is the nearest settlement, and Bannack is almost one hundred and fifty miles away. But cattlemen and ranchers are coming. Some are already here."

"That may be, but there are no churches or schools. We're still just as cut off as we have been since the day we got here. Back home family and friends came over often. Here, we might get a few visitors over a month's time who only want to use the ferry, and they're off again."

"I see," Henry said, "and I sympathize. I can only imagine how difficult this has been for you."

"Not just for me."

"Of course not. But my interest is in you."

He placed his hand under her elbow. She looked up, saw kindness and concern in his eyes, and decided to lead the conversation elsewhere.

"Enough about me for now," she said, smiling. "What were you doing at Fort Benton when James hired you?"

"I had fairly decided to return to the States."

"Do you have aspirations of joining the war?"

"There are many different ways to fight. Many secessionist sympathizers are working in the gold camps west of the divide," Henry said. "I imagine that by now they've arrived at Bannock by the hundreds. The Confederacy needs gold, but the Union will have it."

"There were southerners on the *Emilie* who almost caused trouble until the captain put a stop to it," Electa said. "But enough politics. Do you still plan to go east when you can?"

"It all depends on Dame Fortune. I believe she's smiling on me now."

She blushed, and faced west toward the mountains. The falling sun washed the clouds with its rich gold, which fell on her face and shone in her hair.

"I believe I've found something that I'm afraid I can't live without."

"Oh? And what might that be?" she asked, afraid to look at him.

"You, Miss Electa."

She blushed again. "You compliment me, Mr. Plummer."

"And myself, I'm afraid. Since life is haphazard at best and dangerous at worst, there is little time to mince words. Please call me Henry."

"And please call me Electa," she said, smiling. She began the walk again.

"Tell me about your family. Are they still alive?" she said.

"I believe so. We're seafaring, but as a boy I became inflicted with consumption, which keeps me from making a living on the sea."

"How did you get out West? Through Fort Benton like we did?"

"No, when I turned nineteen, a doctor recommended the Western climate. So, I left for California by way of Panama. It was a hard trip and my health suffered at first, but improved when I reached San Francisco. I worked as a clerk there. When strong enough, I tried mining."

"Well, of course I've heard talk about the gold strikes and all, but you're the first person I've met who has actually been there."

"It's not a huckleberry above a persimmon than anywhere else," he said grinning. And it's not full of churchgoing people. Mostly it's a rough crowd."

"Were you part of that rough crowd?"

"Some. I've made mistakes," he said. "Mostly I just worked hard, but there were times when I had to defend myself."

"I suppose," she said, "that we've all done things that were foolish, or that we're ashamed of, or wish we hadn't done. My speech can pile on the agony if I'm not careful."

"I find that hard to believe."

"Oh, it's true, you can ask Martha," she said, and then added with a smile, "but I wish you wouldn't." They laughed together easily.

"Now it's your turn," he said. "Tell me about Ohio."

"Oh, it's wonderful rich farm country with lots of big trees, which I miss terribly."

"And family?"

"I had two brothers and four sisters. We raised mostly corn and animals until mother died when I was young and father remarried. He then got sick and couldn't help my brothers in the fields. A friend of father's, Mary, came to live with us. She has the same name as mother, but didn't love us like a mother. When I was thirteen, father died and in settling accounts, my brother was fair to Mary but she wasn't satisfied. She sued and got some of the land, but we were all so upset that no one would even live with her."

"That's understandable. Did you live with James and Martha at the time?"

"Yes. But Martha is so forgiving, and felt sorry for Mary being alone, so she asked her to live with us. But when Reverend Reed became the Indian agent and asked James to run this farm, it was all so exciting that I agreed to come along. I'm afraid that none of us were prepared for such change."

"You're different than most women out here."

"How so?"

"You're so, well, unassuming. Innocent."

She turned to face him. "Is there anything wrong with that?" she said, her voice intense. "I happen to be satisfied with my, well, what you call innocence. I consider it to be a Christian virtue."

Her reaction caught Henry by surprise. "Yes, ma'am. I didn't mean," he stammered, "that there is anything wrong with the way you are."

"Of course you didn't," she said, turning away, embarrassed by her display. "You're too kind for that. I apologize for flying at you."

"That's all right," he chuckled. "I've never been called kind before. Even when pushed into a fight, I like to think that I'd rather not. I have a confession to make, and after I say it, if you would rather I take you back to the house and not call on you again, I'll understand."

"I won't believe you could do anything so horrible that it would cause me not to speak to you again."

"I'm a peaceful man when I can be. But sometimes men are forced to violence, like the war, and out here."

"What are you trying to say, Henry?"

"That I have had to kill men to save my own life."

"Oh," she said.

The shadows suddenly seemed longer and the air colder. She shuddered at the thought as well as from the cool air and turned to face him. "I don't care. It doesn't matter. I believe killing is wrong, but I know there are times when it can't be helped." She paused and said, "Do you believe in God?"

"I haven't been to church much."

"I didn't ask you that."

"I haven't thought about it," he said.

"Well, I want you to think about it now. I'm not asking you to believe everything just the way we do, but I do want you to believe in God."

"When James prays, I bow my head. I guess from respect. Not just for him or for what you believe, but respect for something bigger than myself. If you want to call that God, then I suppose I do believe. Besides, I reckon that the river, the trees, the mountains, even we came from Someone bigger than us."

"See, you do believe in God."

Relieved, she smiled at him and he returned it.

"I reckon I do. I just never thought about it."

"Well, I'm glad you did. I apologize for being so pushy about it."

"No, I'm glad you brought it up. I know it's important to you, and I respect that."

"And you respect God, too," she said, smiling.

"Yes I do," he said, and laughed.

"Perhaps we'd better get back to the house before James comes looking for us," she said.

"You're right. It's almost dark and the lamp is lit. But first, let me give you this," he said, holding out a wild pink rose, which she accepted.

"Thank you. That's very thoughtful of you. It smells sweet. I'll dry it so it will last."

They walked slowly, neither of them wanting to reach the house.

"You've been a clerk and a miner," she said. "What else have you done?"

"I partnered in a California ranch near Nevada City with a man named Robinson. We worked a mine together, too. But we split up when I reckoned there was more money to be made in a town business. So I bought a house and started a bakery with a man named Heyer."

"Henry, you? A baker? Really?"

"That's right, the United States Bakery, Henry Plummer, proprietor. Did real well, too. I bought my partner out and worked alone for awhile, but later I thought we should go back into business. We did, but a year later I got out of the bakery business for good."

"Why? It's honest work and you did well at it."

"Yes, but not very exciting. I've found that I truly relish a challenge. The less chance I have to get the job done, the better I like it."

"And what could be more challenging than starting several businesses and more rewarding than making an honest living?"

"Being a lawman."

She stopped again, surprised at the assorted interests of this unusual man. Henry touched her elbow and nodded toward the house to indicate that they should continue.

"I said that I sympathize with your loneliness because I've been homesick myself," he said. "I was so sick for home that by the time I reached San Francisco I had a notion to go back."

"Why didn't you?"

"Well, I reckoned that I came out here for some pretty good reasons. The climate is recommended and I had made good friends. So, I went back to Nevada City and ran for city marshal."

"A marshal!" Electa gasped excitedly, "Did you win?"

"I sure did," he said, laughing.

"Surely that was challenging enough for you?" she asked.

"An elected man can never please everyone, but the action did make up for dry times. After a year of catching robbers and cattle thieves, the Democrats asked me to run for the state legislature."

"That's so exciting! What happened?"

"Well, politics being politics, I lost." He smiled, and having already accepted the fact, raised his hands and dropped them in resignation. "Well, here we are back at your house already. Thank you for the fine walk."

"Thank you for asking me," she said. "You have both flattered and forgiven me, not to mention being the perfect gentleman, which I appreciate."

"You're welcome," he said. "Perhaps we could all go for a wagon ride in the country soon."

"That would be wonderful. I haven't been away from here since we arrived. I'll ask James about it."

They said good night and Electa went inside. It was now dark. James sat reading at the table, while Martha darned socks in her rocking chair.

"How was your walk?" Martha said.

"Wonderful," Electa said dreamily; "He's the perfect gentleman, kind and very capable. Good night." She went into her room and closed the door.

"I'd like to know what he is capable of," Martha said.

"Remember, dear, she is of age and will make her own choices. We have to trust her to follow God's leading in her own life."

In her room, Electa finished her letter.

October 2, 1862

Victoria, our walk was heavenly. I still feel as though I am floating. Henry is kind and a remarkable gentleman. He gave me a lovely wild pink rose, which I shall always cherish. He is the most interesting man I believe I have ever met. If he is not my Prince Charming, I can't imagine anyone more wonderful. I know that God has placed him in my life and I don't dare think what shall happen next.

Sincerely in Christian Love,
Electa

Chapter Nine ~ The Picnic

"Good morning," Electa said as Henry, Joseph, and Jack came in for breakfast. She poured steaming cups of coffee.

"Good morning," Henry replied, and the men sat down at the table.

Henry and Electa's smiles and the obvious happy tone of their voices worried Martha, amused James, pleased Joseph, and angered Jack, who quietly ate biscuits and coffee while keeping to himself. When the men went out to work outside cutting firewood and repairing the compound fence, Henry hauled water from the river so the women could clean, wash clothes, and fix the noon meal. Mary and Harvey played under the table, out of the way. Electa looked forward to meal times and when Henry brought the water instead of Jack or Joseph. Those were opportunities to get to know one another, if only for a few minutes at a time.

Toward mid-day, the aroma of fresh bread began to waft outside. The women chitchatted about a variety of things, but Electa didn't say anything about the walk. Martha's curiosity finally peaked as they set the noon table.

"So, how was your time with Mr. Plummer?" she said.

"Everything I hoped it would be," Electa said. She couldn't help but smile.

"Electa Bryan, tell me what happened before I bust."

Electa paused thoughtfully. "It was a wonderful time with a man who I hope is very interested in me."

"You're not serious," Martha said, incredulous.

"Why not, I'd like to know? You know that I want to start my own family. I don't want to leave you all, but I believe that it will be necessary when the time comes. Besides, I believe God has brought Henry here as an answer to my prayers."

"Well, that is possible, and I know you're more lonely here than I am," Martha said, waving flies away from the table. "But for goodness' sake, you've only spent one evening with the man. You don't really know him. Give yourself time."

"Well, I'm not as forward as all that," Electa teased, "but I am determined to know him as well as I can."

"I assume you'll honor your promise to Mr. Cleveland to walk with him as well?"

"Of course, silly. But do you honestly think he can hold a candle to Henry?" Electa said, laying cloth napkins beside each plate.

"Well, I must admit that he isn't as polished as Mr. Plummer, but shine alone doesn't make a husband," Martha said, holding up a glistening butter knife to make her point.

"No, but understanding, patience, and love do."

"Well," Martha sighed while washing Harvey's hands, "you do seem to have a grasp of the institution," she conceded. "But if you'll take my advice, you won't set one man against the other."

"My duty to each man is as God allows my heart. But only one can have it. And if I do make a commitment to one of them, what goes on between them will be their business."

"And we should all pray for that day," Martha said with a sigh.

~

About a week later, the first light dusting of snow fell during the night, but melted in the morning wherever the sun touched it. After breakfast, Henry went hunting with Joseph. About midmorning after Electa had finished cleaning up, Jack escorted her on a walk even though the day took its time warming up. The cloudless, pretty day didn't lessen the uneasiness between them. Their words were friendly but few. As they neared the house they saw the men returning, descending the plateau to the north.

"I'd better be going in now. Martha needs my help with dinner, and I'm cold," Electa said, smiling. "Thank you, Jack."

Disappointed, he hadn't expected the cold to shorten their time together. He got halfway to the cabin when Joseph opened the gate. Henry rode into the compound.

"Have a nice time?" Henry asked on his way to the barn.

"A little on the short end, thanks to you."

Henry reined his horse and faced him. Steam rose from the heated animal. "We didn't come back to ruin your time with the lady. You know James wanted us back by noon and it'll be that pretty quick. You didn't miss out on much time with the lady."

"How do you know what I missed out on?"

Henry placed his hand on his pistol, leaned forward in the saddle, and lowered his voice. "Be careful, Jack. I'd kill you for that, but I'm afraid your demise would spoil the lady's day. That's my last warning and the God-honest truth." Straight-faced, he lifted the reins and nudged his horse toward the barn. He grinned to himself at Jack's cantankerous mood and thought how much easier it is to catch sweethearts with honey than vinegar. Disgusted, Jack spat tobacco juice on his way to the cabin.

~

The next morning at breakfast, Jack remained in a bad mood. Electa questioned Henry with her eyes while pouring him coffee, but he just smiled at her.

"Morning, Jack," Henry said.

"Humph," Jack replied.

"Since today is Sunday," Electa said, "why don't we all go for a picnic in the wagon? You men get outside to work while the rest of us have been cooped up in here for too long."

James's eyebrows creased while he turned his coffee cup around in his hands.

"I don't think that would be a good idea," Martha said, serving buckwheat cakes. "The miners that James ferried over last week said that the Indians have been killing people."

"We haven't seen any Indians lately," Electa said, pouring more coffee, "and those stories may only be rumors."

"True enough," James said. "We haven't been officially notified of any killings." He knew full well that they probably wouldn't have been notified anyway.

"That doesn't mean it hasn't happened," Martha said.

"But," James said, "a rumor doesn't mean it has, either. We haven't seen any Indians except Iron for several weeks. And I think a picnic would be a good way to spend the day. There's just a skiff of snow and Electa is right; we could all use a picnic."

Henry smiled at Electa, who returned it and nodded an "I told you so."

"And if we find Indians?" Martha said, placing muffins on the table.

"They'll have to have their own picnic," James said, making everyone laugh except Jack, who only gave a slight grin. After breakfast, James invited the men to stay for Bible reading. Jack excused himself to curry his horse.

"While you're at it, would you harness the team to the wagon?" James said.

He knew that a request was as good as done with Jack, who put his hat on and touched the brim in respect before he left. Henry and Joseph also left while the women finished cleaning up, but promised to return for the reading. Henry saw it as a chance to spend more time with Electa. Back inside, the men hung their hats and sat down at the table again. James gathered the children up on his lap. He sat Mary on one leg and Harvey on the other. His Bible lay between them on the table.

"Let us bow our heads in prayer," he said, which everyone did. "Dear God, You know our situation. The Indians have refused to learn everything we've come here to teach them. Help them to know that we want to be friends and that we can help them. Bless our picnic this afternoon with safety. Amen. 'I am the LORD, I change not," he read. "Whatever happens, we should let God be God. That is the one thought I would invite each of us to think about today. Gentlemen, our custom is for each one to share something for which we're thankful, but please don't feel constrained. But if you would like, you may share. Martha dear, would you care to begin?"

She folded her hands, placing them in her lap, smiled, and spoke quietly.

"It's hard for me to trust God at times, but His Word always encourages me. I will try to let God be God more than I have in the past." She grinned, glancing at Electa.

"I'm thankful for answered prayer," Electa said, looking at Henry. "And that encourages me to continue praying."

Henry smiled, which made her blush. Joseph cleared his throat and twiddled his thumbs before he spoke. "I don't have a family of my own anymore, but I appreciate how you treat me like family and let us all eat together. Well, I think it's real nice."

James and Martha grinned at one another. Henry pushed his chair back and crossed his legs, running his fingers back through his reddish-brown hair before speaking.

"I appreciate James rescuing me from the boredom at Fort Benton and giving me something to do," he said. Looking at Electa, he said, "I also appreciate the interest that has been shown in me since I've been here." Electa felt everyone's gaze and looked down at her lap.

"And what are you thankful for, Mary?" James said, bouncing her on his knee.

"For Momma and for Poppa," she said. Embarrassed, she covered her face with her small hands, and they all laughed.

"Let's thank God together," James said. "Thank You, Lord, for the men who have come here to help protect us. Be with us today in the beauty of Your creation. Amen."

The light snow had cooled the crisp autumn air. Billowing white clouds moved slowly across the wide, blue sky. The Indian agent had left a suitable wagon in the barn. A government-issue four-horse ambulance, it had three seats and room in the back to carry baggage, or food for a picnic. Wood posts supported a canvas roof and sides, which could either be tied up to allow a breeze through, or left down for protection from the elements. Henry waited at the wagon to help the women and children up into their seats. He wanted to give Jack the impression that he and Electa had an understanding. Jack sat on his horse pretending not to notice, but when she came out he stole a glance and tipped his hat.

"Ready, Jack? Thank you, Henry," she said after he helped her up.

"My pleasure, Miss Electa," he replied.

Martha and Electa placed blankets across the children's laps while Henry mounted his horse, and Joseph stood waiting at the opened gate.

"Giddyap!" James said, snapping the reins. "If the air gets too cold, we can drop the sides, but you won't see much," he said over his shoulder.

"This is fine," Electa said, wanting to watch Henry, who had staked an immediate claim near her.

They fell into a kind of formation. Henry rode beside Electa and Jack at the rear, who, as he rode by, gave Joseph the definite impression that he was sulking. James had asked Joseph to ride to the front after closing the gate behind Jack.

Electa thought that Henry looked as dashing as any general. Thrilled that he chose to ride by her, goose bumps ran up her neck. The small company headed northwest through the buffalo grass, climbing the plateau north of the compound as they watched for Indians. From there they could see the Sun River as it unwound from the mountains to the west.

"Miss Electa, a picnic was a fine notion," Henry said.

"Thank you," she said, loudly enough to be heard. Her soft voice in the midst of the wagon noises suddenly impressed him with her gentle vulnerability. The realization came over him that she needed looking after, and the desire to protect her welled up from deep within him. She was plain, yet attractive in a simple, honest way. He admired her for having good reasons for believing right is better than wrong. She had said that she had no idea where she was going. She left that up to God. Maybe she was right about God bringing them together. Maybe there was a reason for his being here rather than going back to the States, after all. And maybe he liked thinking this way. It gave him a restful feeling. Caring about Electa felt good, and he grinned. He didn't know why or how, but somehow he knew that his destiny had been settled since meeting her. His daydream stopped suddenly at the sound of a galloping horse behind them. Reining up his horse, he stood upright in the stirrups, looking back just as Jack's horse slid to an abrupt halt between him and the wagon. Henry's horse jumped ahead, almost unseating him.

"What the?" James said, pulling on the reins to stop the wagon. The women and children were startled as well. Jack laughed heartily at his joke, but Henry, obviously annoyed, patted and rubbed his mount trying to settle him.

"What are you about?" Henry demanded, his gray eyes flashing.

"A race," Jack said, grinning.

Chapter Ten ~ May the Best Man Win

"You're crazy," Henry said. "Why should we race? What for?"

Grinning, Jack looked at Electa and back at Henry. "What for?" he echoed. "For the favor of riding beside her for the rest of the day. The loser rides guard from behind."

"Sorry, Jack, but you've already got that job. And I'm already here."

Jack grew serious. "So am I," he said. "In fact, I've already got your place by the lady and I'm not moving. What's the matter? You afraid?" Jack knew he wouldn't stand for that. Daring more with him than he ever had, Jack knew Henry wouldn't pull a pistol in front of the Vails.

"Why don't we leave it up to the lady?" Henry said.

Jack studied her for a moment. "Because she's too much of a lady to put me down, especially in front of you."

Henry scanned the landscape. "All right then, a race it is," he said, angry and embarrassed at his own suggestion. Priding himself on his choice of a mount, he felt he could readily beat Jack.

"Mr. Vail, with your permission," he said.

"I don't see any way around it. She seems to be a worthy prize," he said, and turned around in his seat to grin at her. Electa frowned at him for making his remark and for allowing the race.

"I don't suppose anyone will ask what I think," she said.

"My lands, racing horses on the Lord's Day," Martha joined.

James stood up, looked around, found what he was looking for, and pointed west. "Those two pines are about a quarter mile off," he said. "How about circling them back to here?"

"Done," Jack said.

"Done first," Henry said, and tipped his hat to the women.

"Joseph!" James said, and waved him back to the wagon. "Are you ready, gentlemen?" he said. After getting into position, they both nodded.

"Then go, boys!" he cried. He held the wagon team back as the two men spurred their horses and headed for the pines through the buffalo grass.

"My dear," James said, as the sound of the horse's hooves faded, "there was nothing else to do. Jack wants to prove himself as good a man as Henry in Electa's eyes."

"I see," Martha said. "But I don't think there is any way on earth he can do that."

"No, there isn't," Electa said. "Winning could never make Jack the better man."

The racing men and horses grew smaller, finally going behind the pines and coming out the other side, slowly, it seemed, from the distance.

"Here they come!" Electa cried, and stood up in the wagon with her hands clasped, unable to hide her excitement.

"It won't be the same between them after this," James said.

Electa sat down again, the excitement drained from her face. "It has never been right between them," she said sadly.

They were close now, their horse's sweat shining and sparkling in the sun. Electa smiled again when she saw Henry winning.

"One young man is going to be upset," Martha said.

"He'll take it like a man," James replied.

Henry reined up at the wagon. "Ladies," he said, taking his hat off with a great sweeping motion.

"Hurrah!" Electa cried, clapping her hands gleefully, but her smile faded quickly when she thought of the embarrassment Jack would face. Henry reined his horse to face him as he rode in, spurring the animal over next to Electa. Jack slowed before reaching them and touched the brim of his hat to the ladies as he passed by.

He looked at Henry and said, "The better horse doesn't prove the better man."

"Nothing as fun as a good horse race," Henry replied, and winked at Electa as James smiled and snapped the reins. Joseph spurred his horse ahead while Jack fell in behind once again. Martha was relieved that no Indians joined their picnic. Jack mostly kept to himself, seeming to sulk for the rest of the day, and everyone kept the same formation on an uneventful return to Sun River. Electa wrote Victoria that evening.

Dear Victoria,   November 12, 1862

I pray this finds you fair and well. We are fine although still without some supplies. Oh, to share with you in person what God is doing in my life. Our situation is unchanged except for Henry and I. Our attraction has grown to affection (I hope) so that I'm almost afraid to wonder what will happen next. I have decided to commit myself to Henry if he should so ask. I have a sincere desire to show him the warm affection of a wife, but that future is yet uncertain. Our Lord has brought my Knight. No "Shining Armor," but Henry's character shines brightly enough for me. May God bless and keep you always.

Devotedly, Electa Bryan

~

About a week later, James went to the barn to talk with the men.

"Henry and Jack," he said, "I'm afraid I have some bad news." He looked through the door at the hills as though daydreaming. The men looked at each other and waited. "I didn't know this would happen, but you may as well know now.

With river travel stopped, I can't pay you, myself, or even buy supplies. I thought you should know before we get too far down the road. I still need you, but you're free to go. If you stay I have no idea when, if ever, I could pay you. I want you to know that I'm sorry, and I'll understand if you must leave. Joseph, you were hired first, so you'll be the last one to go if you choose to stay."

Henry and Jack looked at one another again. Henry raised his eyebrows and sighed in resignation. "Well, Mr. Vail, I don't know about Jack, but I'll be moving on. I've got plans, and if I can't make money here, I've got to somewhere else."

"I hope there are no hard feelings," James said.

"No sir, you've been fair all along," Jack said. Henry nodded in agreement and the men shook hands. That evening Henry and Electa walked together again.

"You seem quiet tonight," she said, glancing at him.

"I suppose I am."

"Has something happened?

"It seems that my plans have had to change."

"Would you like to talk about it? You know how interested I am in your plans."

"Well, it's not his fault, but James can't pay us. I want you to know that I'd like to stay on, but I can't. I've got to earn a living that will" he said, stopping and turning to her, "I want to be honest with you."

Her eyes searched his.

"I hope you always will be."

"If anything is to become of us you must know everything," he said. "I told you that I've had to kill to save my own life. It happened that I had to protect a woman from her own husband. Even though he shot at me first and she spoke up for me at the trial, I was convicted of murder and sent to prison. Consumption weakened me there, so my friends wrote the governor, begging for my release. It was granted, and I returned to Nevada City. You know the rest."

She grinned, which puzzled him. "None of that matters to me," she said. "I know who you are inside. You wouldn't kill anyone unless you had to defend yourself, and that's not murder."

"I've thought about us since we first met," Henry said. "I don't know how you feel about me, and I know it seems sudden, but may I ask James for your hand? I want you to be my wife."

She saw honest concern as well as desire in his eyes. "There's no need to ask James. I am of age, you know," she teased.

She took his arm to begin their walk again, but they kissed instead, the soft, long kiss she had dreamed about since the day they first met.

"What will you do?" she said. "Where will you go, and when will you be back?"

"Grasshopper Creek. There are new diggings there where I can make a start for us. I'll come for you in the spring, after the thaw. Will you wait for me?"

"Of course I will."

They walked to the house where they kissed good night.

~

The next morning the men had saddled their horses before breakfast. Electa was unusually quiet while serving and eating. Martha noticed that Electa and Henry exchanged several long looks between them. She feared what that meant. After the meal, the women pulled wool shawls around their shoulders as everyone went outside in the brisk air to see them off. James wrapped the children in a blanket and held them. The whole river bottom was a white wonder as the hoarfrost glistened, clinging to the grass, the trees, the stockade fence, practically everything in sight except the horses that stood ready to carry the two men away. The frost seemed to dare the cool morning sun that was too weak to melt it. They said goodbye in front of the house.

"Men, you have our thanks," James said. "Feel free to come back anytime."

"Thank you, folks," Henry said, mounting his horse. "James, Electa convinced me that Providence took you to Fort Benton to bring me here. I'll thank you for that and for the room and board. Keep fair and well," he said, tipping his hat. "Miss Electa, I'll see you when the snow melts." She smiled and curtsied, which pleased him.

Jack, grim faced, touched his hat-brim and rode through the gate without saying a word.

Chapter Eleven ~ A Shooting in Bannock

Electa and Joseph walked to the gate to watch the men ride away. Iron had heard the men were leaving and waited until they had gone before approaching the gate on his horse.

"I wonder where the chief is going," Joseph said. Electa remained silent. Missing Henry would be hard. Strangely, her heart felt empty, yet full with hope for Henry's return, and their future.

"Iron go, follow men one day, watch for Indians," he said.

"That's good, Iron. I'm sure they'll appreciate that," Joseph said, nodding.

When he was halfway to the river, Electa called out, "Thank you, Iron," and after a moment asked Joseph, "Do you think they'll be all right?"

"Why, sure, Miss Electa," he said, closing the gate. "Neither one's a newcomer to this country; they've both got fast horses, especially Henry; and they're both better shooters than most. Besides, riding together is a lot better than going it alone."

"Yes, I'm sure that's so," she said. She stamped her cold feet on the dirt, making a small sound with her boots. "I won't see him again until spring," she said.

"Do tell," Joseph said, knowing which of the men she meant.

"If you don't mind me sayin' so, you've got quite a spark in your eye for Mr. Plummer, Miss Electa. I'm thinkin' he's got one for you, too."

She smiled, turned, and looked back again at the men who were now far away in the buffalo grass. "No," she said, "I don't mind, since it's true."

"What do you mean, you'll see him again in the spring?"

"He designs on returning then to marry me," Electa said, proud to say it.

"You must be cold. Let's get you to the house, Miss," Joseph said, and they began walking toward the house again.

"I know what Martha and James will say," she said. "They'll say that I don't really know him, nor do I know what I'm doing. But I do. I love Henry, and I'm going to marry him just as soon as he returns."

"I'm sure you will," Joseph said. "You go on inside now, and warm yourself. Thank you for talking to me about Henry. I'd like to think of him as my friend."

"I'm sure you can. I'm sure we all can. Thank you, Joseph," she said, smiling. She went inside, found James and Martha sitting at the table, and went to the stove without taking her coat off, taking in it's warmth.

"Electa, what did Henry mean when he said, 'Until the snow melts'? Is he coming back then?" Martha said.

Electa looked at her sister, her best friend. Martha had watched over her for as long as she could remember. But that time was closing, and the thought of it saddened her and brought tears. Her voice broke when she spoke.

"Yes, to marry me," she said, crossing her arms defensively.

James and Martha sat in stunned silence for a moment, then looked at one another before they studied her again.

"Why are you crying?" Martha said.

"Because I will have to leave you all."

"Electa, are you sure about this?" James said.

"Surely you knew we were growing close," Electa said, sobbing.

"Yes, as friends perhaps, but marriage? That's an awfully big step," he said.

"No greater than coming to this wilderness on faith," she said, taking her coat off and wiping her eyes with a handkerchief. "I know I'm part of this family, and I'm thankful for you all, but it's not the same. I want to start my own family. I'm ready to make a commitment to him and I fully intend to do that when he returns in the spring. I have been asking God to bring someone into my life since we left St. Louis, and Henry and I both believe that God has brought us together. We have talked about many more things than you apparently think we have. Please excuse me, I need to write Victoria. I'll be out in a little while to help with dinner." She went to her room and quietly shut the door. She got out pen, ink, and writing paper, and sat down on the bed.

Dear Victoria,   November 19, 1862

I hope this finds you in good health. We are all fine here but I expect our situation to worsen before spring. The Indians have prevented boats from reaching Fort Benton for some time, adding to our lack of supplies and a bland diet. My beloved Henry is one of two men who left this morning for lack of pay. But I rejoice to say that when he returns in the spring, I shall become Mrs. Henry Plummer. Our love has grown so that we see our future as one. I long to show him the full extent of my love, but for now that must wait. I don't know when this will reach you, but I must share this with someone or my heart will fairly burst. The family thinks my future is uncertain, but we know that there is nothing more certain than a life of faith. When the time comes for me to marry and leave, I will miss them terribly, but they must learn to trust God with my life as I am.

Devotedly, Electa Bryan

~

Several days later, Henry and Jack arrived in Bannock after a quiet but tense trip through the mountains. High hills scattered with sparse buffalo grass and sagebrush towered north and east of the wild young community. Lower hills and flat benches of land stretched to the south. In between the high and low hills, at the bottom of a narrow valley running east to west, lay

Grasshopper Creek and Main Street. They found the place similar to every other mountain gold-rush berg they had seen. Miners had built small crude cabins or lived in caves dug out of the sides of hills, shored up with logs. A wide Main Street had been lined out north of the creek with log buildings on both sides. South of the creek sat a small expanse several hundred yards across. Confederate miners dubbed it Yankee Flat from the number of northern sympathizers that settled there. Henry took a room at the Goodrich Hotel on Main, which sported a saloon and a second-floor porch. During his first few weeks he found gold, staked several claims, and won a number of miners as friends. He soon became known as a composed, polished, and fair man. Many felt he was capable of giving trusted, capable advice, so they took their grievances to him for a fair solution. Word eventually reached Henry that Jack had not been speaking well of him. Some speculated that Jack intended to kill Henry, since he had called him his "meat," insinuating that he could take Henry at any time. One December day after the cold had shut down the placer mines, Henry approached the Goodrich. He stopped as a man came out.

"Jack Cleveland in there?" Henry said.

"Sure enough."

"Much obliged," Henry said and went inside. Jack leaned heavily against the dark walnut bar, obviously fairly drunk, but sober enough to notice Henry's arrival.

"I suppose you think you're the better man," Jack said, not even looking at him.

"Never said that, Jack."

"Well don't, or I'll have to prove you wrong. And for puttin' me down, I'll thank you to keep your distance or I'll settle your hash." Jack put his hand on the butt of his gun, which Henry noticed.

"That's fine as frog's hair with me, as long as it goes both ways," Henry said.

"You bet," Jack said and swaggered toward the door.

"It's just as well that we do keep our distance," Henry said, turning around to watch him leave. "You've had a chip on your shoulder since we came east." Henry knew he would have to deal with Jack sooner or later. He couldn't build a future for himself and Electa as long as Jack damaged his reputation. He reckoned that Jack had better watch his step. Christmas and the first two weeks of 1863 passed coldly for the five hundred or so men, women, and children of Bannock. Henry's gold claims began to pay off; he called a growing number of men his friends, and hoped to be elected marshal. No one could mine until the cold weather broke. Most men occupied their time either by staying close to a warm stove or spent their hard-earned gold dust gambling, drinking, and carousing. Some gathered promising dirt that they planned to work in the spring. Jack continued to boast wherever Henry wasn't found: in the Elkhorn, the Goodrich Hotel and Saloon, and Skinner's Saloon.

On a cold January day in the corner of the Goodrich, the barber stood busily cutting a customer's hair. Jack walked in unsteadily. Anyone could see that he'd been drinking. Henry sat on a low bench by the stove talking quietly with several other men.

"There sits my meat," Jack said with a raised voice, glancing at Henry. "I'm the chief around here, and I'll fight any man who says otherwise. You there, Perkins, when are you going to pay the money you owe me?"

Jeff Perkins, a soft-spoken man who talked ill of no one and minded his own business, sat next to Henry.

"Now Jack, you know I already paid you," Jeff protested.

"Maybe I'll just have to take it," Jack said, and took out his gun as he turned around and pointed the barrel toward Jeff and Henry.

"Let it go, Jack," Henry said casually. "Perkins already paid up. Be satisfied like any reasonable man. Besides, he doesn't have a gun."

Frowning, Jack reluctantly placed the pistol back in its holster. Henry's brow lowered, his eyes fixed in a serious stare at him. "Behave yourself before you regret your actions," he said.

Jack seemed lost in a stupor until he caught Henry's stern look. He cursed, and again took hold of the butt of his pistol. "I'm not afraid of any man in this town," he said, and began to pull the pistol.

"I'm tired of this," Henry said. He rose from the bench, and drew and cocked his pistol. When at full height he fired into the ceiling over Jack's head. The report boomed between the log walls. Men scrambled and ducked under tables or slipped outside to escape possible injury or death. Before Jack could shoot, Henry quickly cocked and fired again, striking him in his side, and the bullet threw him back against the bar. A billow of smoke spread around Henry's pistol. Jack fell to his knees, clutching his ribs and a spot of blood on his shirt.

"You won't shoot me when I'm down?" he gasped.

"No. Get up," Henry said.

Jack slowly stood, clutching his side while trying to raise his pistol with his other hand. Another loud report from Henry's hand produced yet more smoke. The ball struck true and Jack fell to the floor, bleeding. "Uunnhh," he groaned. No one moved to help him. Henry placed one foot on the bench and reloaded his gun.

"You men remember what you saw today," he said, "Jack drew and pointed his pistol at me and Jeff first."

"That's right," Jeff said, wide-eyed. "I reckoned he was going to shoot."

"Who's going to help Jack?" Henry said, looking around the room. The commotion hadn't so much as interrupted the barber's work in the corner. Hank Crawford, a butcher, had heard the shooting and waited outside. After hearing someone drop to the floor, he entered the saloon.

"I'll take him to my place," he said. "Someone take his feet." They picked Jack up between them and shuffled out to the street as Jack hung between them, his coat dragging the ground. The saloon again returned to quiet talk at the bar and around the stove. An hour later Hank returned. "Henry, Jack said you would get me his blankets," he said. A short heavy man with brown hair and beard, he considered Jack his friend.

"All right," Henry said, and they left together.

"Did Jack say anything about it?" Henry said, as they crossed the street.

"He said what was between you and him was nobody's business. He said to me, 'Poor Jack has got no friends. He has got it, and I guess he can stand it."

"I had every man's right to shoot him," Henry said. "It's good he said nothing against me, for if he had, I would kill him in his bed."

Jack died that evening and Hank arranged to have him buried. The shooting wasn't news but Jack's death was. The general opinion was that he deserved it. Though Jack was a sour, surly, drunken horse trader, some still said Henry should be tried for murder. The next morning at breakfast in the Goodrich, Henry overheard talk about another incident.

"I heard shots last night, but it was too cold to go out."

"What happened?"

"Charlie Reeves had a disagreement south of town with his squaw's daddy, the Bannock chief. Charlie and two friends, Moore and Mitchell, got drunk and shot up the Injun camp. They wounded two white men and killed another."

"They should've been more careful," a man said. "Somethin' should be done."

Henry left the Goodrich and found the three men at the end of the street at Mitchell's place saddling their horses.

"Men," Henry said, "you shouldn't have been so careless. There's talk of you paying for it."

"You're one to talk, Plummer. You're in the same wagon as us," Reeves said, and they mounted their horses. "I've heard talk of you hanging for murdering poor Jack Cleveland. If you value your hide you'll leave with us, and devil take the hindmost."

Henry remembered that the last time he had been unjustly accused, he had been sent to prison, and said, "It's hard to argue against experience."

"Then meet us at Rattlesnake Creek," Reeves said. They spurred their horses and rode away through the cold air, leaving him standing alone in the street.

Chapter Twelve ~ On The Run

An hour later Henry caught up with the three men as they warmed themselves around a fire.

"We're being followed," Henry said. "I could see your smoke for half a mile. I know now I shouldn't have left town."

"I don't want to hang for a drunken mistake," Reeves said.

"Neither do we," Moore said, looking at Mitchell, who nodded in agreement.

Henry thought they looked scared as rabbits. "A posse can be unreasonable," he said, "so we'll have to force them to take us back for trial."

"But all they have is a miner's court," Reeves protested.

"Then that will have to do," Henry said. "It's better than a rope. We'll ride up that canyon until we reach those rocks. When they get there I'll kill any man who shoots at them. I'll do the talking and tell them how we see it." He kicked the fire out and they rode for the narrow canyon. Ten minutes later they led their horses up a narrow trail and hid behind large rocks. "Remember to keep quiet and no shooting," Henry said. Soon enough, they heard horses plodding, leather saddles creaking, and men's voices, so he gave the three men behind him a silent warning. The half dozen riders came into view.

"Every man of you stop there," Henry called out.

"Who's out there and what do you want?" the rider in front answered.

"Your word that if we give ourselves up, we'll get a fair trial."

The chasers spoke to one another quietly.

"You know we've got a miner's court."

"Good enough," Henry answered.

"All right then. Come out meek like good sons of the South and you'll get your trial."

Henry led the way. "I'm no seccesh," he said when he reached them.

"Henry Plummer," the man said, recognizing him. "No, I guess you're not."

They rode in silence and arrived in Bannack as the sun set behind scattered clouds splashed with brilliant red-orange. Henry's thoughts went back to similar sunsets at Sun River Farm and walks with Electa. He knew he had made a foolish miscue that made him look guilty and tied him to men who had committed murder. His unwise act angered him. Though very cold outside, a small crowd met them in the street. The leader of the group spoke before the chasers and their captives dismounted.

"We want them hung before they can shoot anybody else," the man said.

"Folks, we promised these men they'd get a miner's trial if they came back peacefully. It's getting late. I think we should try Plummer tonight, since he's a different case, and won't take as long, and Reeves, Moore, and Mitchell tomorrow. What do you say?"

The crowd agreed. Once inside, a volunteer picked juror's names out of a hat and elected Hank Crawford, the butcher, who had cared for Jack Cleveland, as sheriff. Henry envied him for that. Crawford's first official act was to ask Henry why he left town.

"I am guilty of an act of very poor judgment in leaving. But I'm not afraid because I'm innocent of any crime," he said. "I shot Jack in defense of myself and Jeff Perkins, who had no gun. I place myself at the mercy of the court and trust that my name will be vindicated of any crime."

The judge, a short, rugged-looking red-haired Irishman, said in his brogue, "Anybody here see the shooting?" A half dozen men raised their hands. "Well, did it happen as Mr. Plummer said?" They nodded in unison. "Mr. Plummer, you know better than to leave town after something like this. Let this be a warning to every mother's son not to repeat your mistake. Don't do it again. You are hereby released and not charged with murder."

Afterward, James Morley, one of the jurors, approached Henry outside on the street.

"Congratulations on being let go, Plummer," he said. "Cleveland had it coming."

"I'm a patient man," Henry said, "but every man has his limit and Jack met mine. I'm not proud of killing him. I liked Jack. We could have been friends if he'd allowed it."

"Strange how a man's past can follow him," Morley said. "I didn't know that Jack ran with Watkin's gang in California, but someone here recognized him, and he reaped what he sowed."

"I knew he ran with that bunch," Henry said. "But a man has a right to keep his friends and his past to himself. Jack wasn't wanted when I kept the law in California. We hooked up on the trail and came here together, but as far as I know, he didn't turn bad until we reached Bannock. More than a few men said he'd been laying for me."

"I'm on Mitchell's jury tomorrow," Morley said. "They shouldn't have shot into that Indian camp. I don't expect they'll fare as well as you."

"I wonder," Henry said.

They didn't. Nathaniel Langford volunteered for jury duty and insisted on the death penalty but didn't get his way. Mitchell was found guilty of manslaughter in the first degree, but only banished for two years beyond one hundred miles of the mines.

Reeves and Moore were tried separately the following day and met the same fate. After warmer weather they were to be banished from every gold camp for six hundred miles and all their property confiscated. About a week after the trials, Henry sat eating breakfast at the Goodrich Hotel when Hank Crawford, the new sheriff, entered the room.

"Mind if I sit down?" Crawford said.

"How goes the fight?" Henry said, ignoring the question and continuing his meal.

"I've never fired a gun at a man, have no experience, and didn't want the job, yet they still elected me sheriff," Crawford complained. "I'm no gunman, and men don't respect me. It seems all I do is go back and forth between saloons to break up fights. I don't even like the job."

"All part of being a lawman. You should have turned it down. Everyone will go back to work when the thaw comes," Henry assured him. "Why don't you resign?"

"You'd like that, wouldn't you, Plummer? Then you could volunteer for the job."

"I might," Henry said grinning. "By the way, I'd like my gun back."

"Can't. I already sold it with the others."

Henry hesitated for a moment and looked squarely at him.

"Then I'll ask the miner's court to have you get it back."

"Go ahead, but someone has to pay for feeding those three birds during trial."

That day, Henry went to the court, which ordered Crawford to return all the guns, even to the men who were to be banished in the spring. That forced him to pay for all costs of the trial including the prisoner's food. Hank had hard feelings about that, but Henry didn't much care. Long, cold weeks of idleness and the crowded public buildings wore on the patience of most men. A few mutual friends brought Henry and Hank together in the Goodrich to talk about their differences.

"I'd like to be friends, Hank," Henry said.

"We can try," Hank said, and they shook hands.

But the dispute wasn't as settled as Henry thought. Hank was afraid of what might happen to him, perhaps because of Jack Cleveland's death, and the fact that Henry was so proficient with a gun. Henry continued his friendly attempts through the cold winter weeks.

"Crawford, it's about time we acted like we mean to be friends," Henry said. "If you don't want to be around me, then we can at least act like decent strangers."

"All right. I suppose that would be best," Hank agreed.

But in early February, some of his friends told him they had seen Henry outside Hank's butcher shop. The only reason Plummer might be there was to watch him, they said, so they warned him to keep up his guard, which he did. Henry entered Hank's butcher shop a week later.

"Crawford, I hear you've been spreading talk about me and a squaw. What of it?"

Behind the rough-hewn counter, Crawford sunk a meat cleaver into a large hunk of beef on a chopping block.

"Get out of here, Plummer," he said. "I may not be as good as you with a gun, but I'm no match with this," he said, patting the cleaver's handle.

"You know I'm promised to be married," Henry said. "I'm not going to let anyone ruin my reputation. Leave that knife where it is and come out from there. I'll set my pistol aside and we'll see who the better man is with our fists."

"We both know you'll beat me to a pulp," Crawford said.

"Then I'll give you a fair chance in a duel. Be in Peabody's Saloon in an hour."

Henry left, and Hank sent for Harry Phleger, a large friendly miner, to help him. A nearly deaf man known as Deaf Dick, along with a few other friends, went to Peabody's with Henry. Phleger greeted them with peace offers to drink when they arrived, but all refused.

"Well, Dick," Phleger said loudly, "you'll drink anyhow."

"Not with any coward," Dick replied, looking at Crawford.

Crawford swung a fist at him for that, but Dick backed away too quickly. In the next instant Henry handed his pistol to Dick. Crawford, wanting to be as unarmed as Plummer and seeing that Dick had a gun, quickly gave his own pistol to Phleger.

"Am I to be shot now?" Crawford said, standing up straight and stiffly facing Henry.

Still trying to play peacemaker, Phleger stepped in between Henry and Hank and said, "Who would do that, Hank?" Droplets of sweat ran down Hank's face. Only Henry appeared relaxed.

"Plummer, I suppose," Crawford said weakly.

Phleger began to raise his gun, but Henry, quick as a cat, grabbed his arm before he could get it up. Phleger turned into a better position, grabbed Henry, and swung him around, throwing him to the floor. Henry got up slowly and brushed himself off.

"Come on, Crawford, it's time to leave," Phleger said, and they backed out the door on their way to a room that Crawford slept in at the back of his butcher shop.

"Plummer's going to kill me, I know it," Crawford said.

"I don't believe he's that kind of man," Phleger said. "Besides, you shouldn't have spread those stories. A lot of men would kill you for doing that, but not Henry. He could have killed me for pulling my pistol, but didn't. He knew I wouldn't have fired."

"You won't leave me, not now, not tonight," Crawford pleaded.

"I'll watch the front, and you watch back here," Phleger said, "but I'm telling you he won't come."

He was right. He guarded the front of the store against Crawford's imagined attacker and kept the fire burning in the stove. He heard Crawford weep himself to sleep and pitied the man. Phleger left at sunrise, and several days later Henry approached him on the street.

"Phleger, our blood ran pretty hot the other day," he said. "No hard feelings?"

"Not from me," Phleger said. "But Crawford is another story."

"About Crawford, will you stop by his place and tell him that I'll drop the whole thing if he will? I expect him to act like a gentleman and respect my privacy as well as my reputation."

Phleger agreed and did so, but Crawford, proud and jealous of Henry, only said, "He or I must die or leave the camp."

Two days later, Henry thought his chances at reconciliation with Crawford would be better if he talked to him in person, but carried a rifle to show his readiness for trouble. He waited outside Crawford's shop so they could talk in the open where everyone could see. Standing across the street in the warm sun, Henry placed one boot on a wagon spoke and rested the rifle on his knee in plain view. Several of Crawford's friends were inside.

"Look at this," one of them said, pointing at Henry. Hank went to the window, peered out with his dark eyes, and said, "He's come to kill me for sure."

"What are you going to do about it? You can't stand against him in a gunfight," the man said. "No one would blame you for making things a little more even."

Crawford got his double-barreled shotgun out of the back room. He looked out the window before slowly opening the front door. Henry caught the movement. Crawford raised the heavy gun as fast as he could and fired just as Henry ducked, twisting his body away from the blast.

Chapter Thirteen ~ A Broken Engagement?

Though Henry tried to avoid the blast, the force of the shot knocked him down. Cyrus Skinner ran to help him. Henry cursed the man who had shot him as searing pain ran down to his wrist, which he ignored. He had to. Back on his feet, his right arm hung useless while blood dripped onto his pants and the ground. He faced Crawford's place.

"You're a coward, Crawford!" he shouted. "Fire, since you don't have the nerve to come out."

Crawford's gun boomed again. Skinner ducked while Henry stood his ground in the street. Crawford's second shot missed completely. He panicked, dropped the now empty shotgun, turned, and ran through his place and out the back door.

"Take that to my room, will you?" Henry said to Skinner, nodding toward his rifle. He drew a pistol with his left hand.

"Crawford left out the back," a voice from inside called out.

"Tell him he has two weeks to find the nerve to meet me in a fair fight."

"Henry, you'd better let me wrap that arm," Skinner said. "You're bleeding like a stuck pig."

Crawford didn't stop until he reached Charlie Wadam's cabin and pounded on the door.

"Who is it and what do you want?" a muffled voice said through the door.

"It's Crawford. I need help."

Wadam gave him leave to enter. Once inside, he quickly fastened the wood latch. Turning to face his benefactor, he saw shadows across the dirt floor cast by a single lamp. He smelled coffee. Like every other cabin and dugout in Bannock, its few furnishings were functional yet simple. A frying pan and canned goods sat on crates by the stove. A few clothes hung on nails in a corner. A buffalo robe lay spread on the ground beside the bed. Wadam sat on a box by the stove in the half dark.

"Plummer's going to kill me. I need a place to hide," he said.

Wadam thought for a moment. "Have you a gun?" he said.

"No," Crawford replied, shaking his head.

"All right, I'll help you," he said. "For two reasons. Because my family isn't here and to protect Plummer's reputation. I don't choose my friends politically, like too many do around here. Cleveland had it coming and the good Lord knows you do, too."

Crawford got his point. Wadam continued to preach while hiding him behind sacks of flour in a corner.

"I don't know all about the difficulty between you two, but Plummer is a good man and I count him a friend. If he shows up and you fire on him, I'll kill you myself. He's helped more than a few men in this dig. You picked the right place to hide; I'll give you that. Some would just hand you over or shoot you themselves, but I won't hand Plummer any more trouble. You keep quiet, and I'll fetch your brother after dark."

Skinner and a doctor of sorts, a gray-haired man with a limp, helped Henry to his hotel room. Skinner tossed Henry's holster on a corner chair on their way to the bed.

"Lay him down and raise his arm to stem the bleeding," the doctor said. "Light that lamp if you don't mind, Cyrus." The lamplight cast a yellow tone on the walls and the three men.

"How bad is it, Doc?" Henry said.

"Don't know yet. Cyrus, hold that good arm down by his side and the bad arm above his head, flat down on the bed."

He did so. Henry closed his eyes while the doctor washed the blood off with a wet rag and found the wound.

"Mr. Plummer, I'm sure there's still a ball in your arm somewhere. I'll have to probe in order to find it. Cyrus, fetch that bottle under the bed and give Henry some medicine."

Cyrus lifted Henry up somewhat so he could drink as much as he wanted. Henry took several swallows from it, and Cyrus laid him back down.

"Go ahead," Henry gasped. "I can stand it."

Henry's wet face, cast with a yellow pall of lamplight, became tight and creased. The doctor frowned, and felt for the ball with an instrument.

"I advise you to allow me to remove this arm. Judging from the swelling, it's damaged from the elbow all the way down to your wrist."

"I'm afraid my future won't allow that," Henry replied, breathing hard. "I've always healed well except for the consumption. I expect this will, too."

"And I expect that either one or the other will end your life, my boy. One sooner than the other."

"So be it," Henry said. "But the arm stays on."

"Maybe you'd better listen to him," Cyrus said. "It'd be better than dyin'."

The doctor poured whiskey on the wounds, his frown intact.

"Tarnation, man!" Henry said. "Warn a body before you set him on fire."

Cyrus bore down on his arm to keep it still.

"Young man, it's my opinion that those who live by the sword will most certainly die by it. When the sword does its damage, it's my duty to patch up the wounds. But only the wounded can feel the pain."

"Well, I'm doing a fine job of that."

~

Henry carried his arm in a sling for several weeks while the sun's heat grew stronger and daylight hours increased. Mining started back up along the north side of the creek where the sun thawed the ground. One morning, Cyrus grabbed a chair and joined Henry for breakfast at the Goodrich. His behavior reminded Henry of Jack Cleveland. Cyrus shoved a corner of his napkin down the front of his shirt. Henry always opened his and laid it on his lap.

"I hear tell Crawford's brother slipped him out of town the night you two had your fooferaw," Cyrus said.

Henry swallowed a bite of steak. "He was fortunate that his brother had that discretion," he said.

"They say we should elect another sheriff," Cyrus said. "Word is out that you've got more sense and gumption than most."

"Cyrus, who does all this telling and spreading the word?" Henry said, grinning, glad to hear the favorable report.

Cyrus drank his coffee and ordered more before answering.

"You know a body can go anywhere and hear talk," Cyrus said. "Word is that the election will be in about a month. Should I let it out that you're running for sheriff?"

"I'd like to head north right now and marry Miss Electa Bryan, but the weather won't allow it for at least a month, probably until after the election. We'll get the mine going before I go, too." Cyrus smiled at that.

Henry's arm continued to improve, although his wrist and elbow were stiff. He thought of Electa often. His partnership in the mine had made him a successful businessman. He planned to buy a cabin before leaving for Sun River, and of course the election would be settled by then too. Mining success, property, the possibility of a position of respect as an elected official in the community, and finally, marriage. Everything life had to offer was finally coming to him. While he waited, he wondered how Electa fared.

~

Naturally, spring had arrived at Sun River Farm as well. Electa hoped for Henry's soon arrival while thriving in a love for him that refused to be suppressed. Everyone was glad for her high spirits and good moods, but Martha's reservations and doubts continued to dampen her relationship with Electa. It seemed to Electa that the subject of conversation somehow always returned to the engagement. One evening during the last week of May, Martha sat at the kitchen table darning socks while Electa read *Harper's Monthly Magazine*. James and Joseph had retreated to the front porch. A doughy yet tangy aroma from a bowl of sourdough permeated the house. Martha broke the silence.

"Electa, I simply can't get this fear for your future out of my heart," she said.

"I do appreciate your concern for my welfare, but you're wrong about Henry."

"Since those men came through with those awful tales," Martha said, "I'm afraid you'll ruin your life if you marry him. What if the stories are true?"

"They may very well have been talking about another Henry Plummer for all we know," Electa said half teasing, not caring whether they had been or not. "They might as well have been, for all I care."

"You must care about your future," Martha said. "After all, it's only because I love you that I want what's best for you."

"And what if Henry is best for me? You don't know that he isn't. Honestly, I don't know how we shall ever get past this painful subject between us. I know what Henry is on the inside, where it matters. I know what he's done and why, so I don't see how anything you might say could possibly change my mind."

Martha sighed, searching for an answer, but found none.

~

Another awkward week passed. Never before had there been an invisible wall between them. It now seemed strangely inevitable, like the melted snow rushing down from the mountains swelling the Sun River.

"The river has been too high and fast to run the raft across," James said one morning. "But if anyone comes through now, I might be able to get them across."

After breakfast he decided to make a closer inspection of the river's condition. About halfway there he heard a voice calling his name. He stopped and listened, and finally decided that it came from across the river.

"James Vail! Over here, James!"

Looking closely, he recognized Francis Thompson.

"Hello, Francis! Wait there!" he called and ran back to the house. "Martha, Electa!" he panted, bursting through the door.

"James, what is it?" Martha said, surprised.

"Across the river," he said haltingly, as he sat down at the table to catch his breath. "It's Francis Thompson."

"Francis!" Electa said. "He's come back! How wonderful to see him again."

"I wanted you to know as soon as possible. I'll get Joseph to help bring him across," James said and left to get him.

Both James and Martha wondered what Francis would think of Electa's plans. Martha determined to speak with James about the matter, but in the meantime she didn't think it would hurt to propose a possible solution to Electa.

"Dear, you know what a good friend Francis has been to us all," Martha said.

"Yes, of course. Why do you mention it?"

"Because I think he should be asked about our problem. After all, he is neutral and open-minded. I for one am willing to accept his opinion. Will you promise to break your engagement to Henry if Francis thinks it best?"

Chapter Fourteen ~ To Marry, Or Not?

Electa bit her lip as she thought.

"All right," she said. "If he thinks it best, I will. But only if you, too, are willing to accept his opinion in the matter. If he supports me, then you are to support me as well."

Martha thoughtfully considered Electa's counteroffer.

"All right," she said. "I'm willing if you are. But you know we're only so concerned because we love you and want what's best for you."

"And you know how much I love you and appreciate your concern," Electa said.

They smiled and hugged. Electa determined to trust God more than ever. She knew He had brought Francis back to them for some reason. She also knew that He had brought Henry into her life. A Bible verse came to her mind, which says, "And we know that all things work together for good to them that love God." She knew she loved God, so it was a simple matter to trust Him to work everything together for her good.

At the riverside, it was still too dangerous to use the raft to cross. James went upstream and threw a rope across the brown swirling water to where it could float downriver. Joseph then wrapped their end around the base of a large cottonwood tree at the river's edge to either keep it tight or to give Francis slack as needed. Across the river, Francis held a willow branch and reached out over the water to seize the rope, which he then tied around the saddle horn. He waved to them that he was ready. Urging the horse down the bank, Francis wondered how he and the animal would fare if either the rope or the saddle broke or even if the saddle somehow detached from the horse. The men worked diligently to keep up the slack. Finally Francis made it safely across, wetter and wiser for the experience.

"James!" he said, smiling as he dismounted, "It's good to see you again!"

They shook hands and slapped each other on the back.

"And who is this?" Francis said, nodding at Joseph.

"Francis Thompson, meet Joseph Swift, our helping hand."

"Hello, Mr. Thompson."

"Nice to make your acquaintance, Joseph."

"We'd better head for the house. There are four women there who can't wait to see you," James said.

Curious, Francis said, "Four women?"

"That's right," he said, smiling. "Martha and Electa are so excited to see you that they're beside themselves."

They laughed as James coiled the rope. He wondered to the gate if he should mention Electa and Henry, but thought better of it. It really wasn't Francis's concern, and he wanted to talk about it with Martha first. The women came outside to greet Francis, squealing with delight as they ran to him.

"Ladies, ladies!" he said, overwhelmed by their excited hugs. "I've never had such a welcome!"

"Well, we're starved for news from the outside world!" Martha said.

"Oh, I thought you wanted to see me!" he teased.

They laughed as Joseph excused himself to return to work. They went inside, where Francis changed into dry clothes and Martha cut him a slab of fresh pie. There was no coffee left. He told them of his travels, after which Electa took the children outside for a walk. Martha saw her chance. She caught James's eye and raised her eyebrows in a questioning look. He nodded, giving his assent.

"Francis, I'm sorry that there's only water to drink."

"This is just fine, Martha. Thank you."

"We have something we'd like to ask you," James said, pushing his chair away from the table and crossing his legs. "We don't mean to push our problems onto your shoulders, but we've come to a place where we need an outside opinion. We count you as a friend, and we'd be obliged if you would help us."

"I'd be honored to do my best for you," Francis said.

James related how he had gone to Fort Benton and hired Henry and Jack, that Electa and Henry had apparently fallen in love, and of their plans to marry when he returned, which could be any day.

"He seems to be a fine young man," Martha said. "He's polite, charming, and well-mannered. We have trusted him without reservation. But we've heard disturbing accounts of his past, and frankly, we're afraid."

"What is it that you're afraid of?" Francis said.

"That the rumors are true," she continued, "and that marriage to such a man will simply ruin her life. Surely there are better prospects than a man whose future is as uncertain as his past. I've tried to talk some good judgment into her, but she is convinced that she's doing the right thing, even fulfilling God's will for her life. You know how we love her, so we feel somewhat responsible for her future. I'm afraid, that for good or bad, I've come to feel more like a mother to her than a sister. But," she sighed, "thankfully, I have gotten her to agree to abide by your considered advice."

Conversation stopped as they all stared blankly at the table, as though their problem had been set out like some mesmerizing visible object.

"I see," Francis said, breaking the silence and tapping his fingers on the table. "I'm afraid I'm not as impartial as you think because I already share your concerns."

James and Martha exchanged uneasy glances.

"I came across a pack train while on the trail. The men told me about a young outlaw named Henry Plummer who is now living in Bannock. They said that he recently killed a man there named Jack Cleveland."

Martha gasped. James looked stunned.

"What's wrong?" Francis said. "Did you know Mr. Cleveland?"

"Yes. Yes, we did," James said slowly. "I hired him at the same time as Henry, and they went to Bannock together."

"Oh, I'm sorry. Well, when Electa hears of my prejudice, she may not be inclined to follow my advice. Even when she learns of Mr. Cleveland's death."

"You may be right about that," James said.

"What did Joseph think of Mr. Plummer?" Francis asked.

"You will have to ask him," James replied. "Would you like me to get him?"

"No, I'll go out to him. Then I'd like to speak with Electa. The sooner the better, I think, but I want to get another opinion about Mr. Plummer first."

Francis went outside to the barn and found Joseph there feeding the horses.

"Hello, Joseph. I'd like to speak with you if I may."

"Sure, Mr. Thompson. What about?"

"Mr. Plummer. I understand you spent quite a bit of time with him."

"Yes, sir. I count him as a friend."

"Oh? And what about the stories?"

"You mean about him being a killer and a convict? I know he killed a man in self-defense; he told of that. And that he spent time he shouldn't have in prison, too. If he hadn't had so many friends writing the governor to free him because he was so sick, he'd still be there. Or more likely, dead by now."

"So you don't believe all the stories you've heard about him," Francis said.

"Mr. Plummer told me some himself, and Miss Electa told me the rest. She said he told her the truth and she believed him. And I believe them both. They're my friends, and friends are few and far between around here."

He went back to feeding the horses. Francis thanked him. Impressed by Joseph's loyalty, but unconvinced, Francis remained anxious on his way back to the house and his meeting with Electa. He knocked before entering the house, entered at James's consent, and shrugged at Martha's inquiring look. Martha knocked on Electa's door.

"Electa, will you please come out?"

"What is it, Martha?" she said, opening her door.

"Francis would like to have a talk with you. Why don't you show him around the compound?"

"All right," she said, looking at him. "Let me get my coat."

"What's on your mind?" she said as they walked away from the house.

"Electa, this may sound surprising coming from me, but I want you to reconsider your plans to marry Mr. Plummer."

She stopped, alarmed at his suggestion, and her mouth fell open.

"You too?" she said. "It didn't take Martha very long to influence you, did it? You haven't been here an hour and she has you convinced that he's the Devil himself."

"Electa, please understand. I didn't hear about him from Martha first. I met some men on the trail who told me about him. I don't know him from Adam, and didn't know at that time that you do. They said he's an ex-convict, called him an outlaw, and said he's living in Bannock."

"I don't care what anyone says about him. I love him and know that he loves me. I have more faith in him than any man I've ever known. The stories you've heard shouldn't be believed. You'd know that if you knew Henry. He's simply not capable of the things they say he's done."

"Any man is capable of anything if push comes to shove," Francis said.

"I'll never believe that of Henry, even if it's true. I live for the day when I'll see him again and we're married. I could never be happy unless I marry him."

"Electa, I've got some bad news."

"About Henry? Is he all right?"

"I'm afraid he killed another man you know after they left here. Jack Cleveland."

She gasped as Martha had, again shocked at his words, covering her mouth with her hands. She knew that Jack had cared for her too. She began to walk again and he joined her. He thought he should press on, using the situation as well as his influence to sway her mind.

"Even if it was a fair fight," Francis said, "you know he's a man marked by violence. You believe that a man who lives by the sword dies by the sword, don't you?"

"I'm afraid I do," she said, her voice barely audible.

"Then you know that he can't have a good end coming to him. Let him go. God will give you a better man. You deserve one." He could see by her expression that his prediction bothered her. "Take your time before you make such an important, final decision," he urged. "Why not go to Fort Benton and take the steamship back to the States? You'll have time to think about what you should do, and by this fall, if you still love him, and if he still loves you, then he could join you there."

"I know that I agreed to abide by your opinion," Electa said, "and may the good Lord forgive me for not keeping my word, but the best I can do is to consider what you've said. I'll make no more promises concerning Henry when I've already made a promise to him."

"All right Electa, if that's the best you can do, then I suppose that you, Martha, and Henry will just have to live with that," he said, smiling.

Together, they walked back to the house, and as they reached it, Joseph called from the barn.

"Mr. Thompson!"

"I'll go on inside," Electa said. "It seems Joseph needs you."

He touched the brim of his hat as she left him.

"Yes, Mr. Swift," he said and met Joseph halfway to the barn.

"Mr. Thompson, may I be so bold as to ask what your plans are?"

"Well, I suppose that would be all right. My plans are no secret. I hope to meet the Shreveport at Fort Benton. She's bringing goods for a store I plan to open."

"I see. At Fort Benton or Bannock?"

"I don't know. I've not been to Bannock yet. Perhaps there, if I can find an appropriate place and it works out."

"Good. Then you'll meet Henry and decide for yourself what kind of man he is."

Francis simply nodded and returned to the house. Inside, he told the Vails about Electa's decision and renewed confidence in Henry, which distressed them. Electa had gone to her room to write Victoria even though she had no idea when the letter would be posted or reach her.

Dear Victoria;   May 22, 1863

I pray this finds you well. Everyone is fine here in spite of a diet lacking in sugar, tea, coffee, and spices. James has yet to convince any Indian to stand behind a plow, and ships cannot get through to bring us either pay or supplies, so Sun River Farm may not succeed after all.

I hope to be married by the time this reaches you. Francis Thompson arrived with a fairly set opinion against Henry based entirely on rumor, which, I regret to say, angers me. The justice of his logic escapes me, yet my faith in Henry never will. I understand his concern, as well as that of Martha and James, but surely you of all people understand. I promised Martha I would abide by Francis's decision, but I find his bias perfectly unacceptable, and feel my release from such a promise is justified. Pray for us in such uncertain times.

Yours Devotedly,
Electa Bryan

Chapter Fifteen ~ The New Sheriff

Over the next month things settled down a bit. It reminded Henry of a calm before the storm on the ocean. To him, it seemed as though the little town was resting before a scrap. His arm continued to mend, probably because he worked it every day. He hired men for the season and got them started working his claims. Now that Crawford had left the country, Henry had nothing but friends.

The day before Bannock's Election Day, he went to see an unoccupied house he had heard about. He could easily afford it. A simple cabin, the one-room mud and slate-roofed square of logs sat on Second Cross Street. The door hinges creaked as he pushed the door open, allowing sunlight to pour in. With his arms folded, he turned around in the middle of the dirt floor and considered the place. It smelled of dust and dried pine, fresh and old at the same time. A small black iron stove sat near a table underneath corner shelves, its vertical pipe inserted in the roof. A rough-hewn bed sat in a corner. He imagined what Electa could do with the place.

"Not a castle, but it's a start," he said. "Can't bring her to a hotel room."

Closing the door behind him, he said to the emptiness, "Only a woman could cheer you up." On his way to see the owner he passed Cyrus Skinner smoking a cigar in front of his Elkhorn saloon, named for a large set of antlers hung over the door.

"How's the arm today, Henry?" Cyrus said.

"Fine, Cyrus. How's business?" Henry replied.

"Who you gonna vote for?" Cyrus teased, ignoring the polite question.

"What do you think?" Henry said.

Cyrus laughed loudly in his crude way. Henry grinned and felt confident that he would win. Thinking back, he reckoned that his good fortune turned up the day he and Jack met James at

Fort Benton. That blasted Jack! Why did he have to be so contrary? He and Crawford had been cut from the same cloth. He found Mr. Allen eating at the Goodrich and sat down at his table.

"Have you seen the house, Mr. Plummer?"

"Yes, I have."

"What do you think? Will it suit your needs?"

"I want a place over on Yankee Flat but will have to wait since none are available. Yours is the best there is, so here's payment," Henry said, tossing a small leather poke of gold dust on the table.

"There you are, Mr. Plummer, signed and legal," Allen said and read:

"Received of Henry Plummer for $25.00 consideration, lot No. 10, Second Cross Street, Bannock City, May twenty-third, 1863. Signed, Augustus V. Allen.' Hope you enjoy the place with your new bride."

"Thank you, sir, I'm sure we will."

"I hear you'll soon fetch her?"

"After the election. Can I depend on your vote, Mr. Allen?"

"Certainly. And if I may say so, since that unfortunate scrape with Crawford, you have behaved with the utmost propriety. That other shooting with Cleveland couldn't be helped either. Weren't you two friends at one time?"

"I thought so."

"You'll do as sheriff, but you'll need some good men for deputies."

"If I'm elected the town will trust my judgment. Believe me, my men will have enough grit to get the job done."

"The best of luck to you, sir," Allen said, and they shook hands.

"Thank you, sir, and likewise," Henry said, and picking up the receipt, he excused himself. He went outside, sat down on a chair, tilted it back against the wall, and thought about the election. It would be held in the lobby behind him since it had been decided that voting should be done in a place befitting the honor of the first election in Bannock. Besides, it was the largest place in town and would accommodate ballot boxes, election officials, and voters.

He had to plan what he would do if elected. He reckoned that the town obviously needed a jail. He could probably raise enough money to build one on subscriptions if enough civic-minded folks supported such a project. After the election he would send an order for barred windows on the first freight team that left for Salt Lake City. Freight wagons arrived almost every day now.

Walking Main Street he did some politicking, shaking hands with the men, and asking for votes. He took a trail on the south side of Main down to Grasshopper Creek to encourage miners to cast their votes. At the edge of the stream he found several, and they stopped working when he approached.

"Men," he said, "you owe it to yourselves and the rest of the town to vote. We need someone who will do the job day or night, and I'm your man. I'm experienced and would like to have your vote."

He gave the speech to every bunch of men he could find on the creek until dark. Then he went to each saloon asking for more. After breakfast on Election Day, he voted before going next door to Cyrus's saloon, a wood building with a plank floor. Its most ornate feature was an old walnut bar, simple compared to most. Hauled in by a freight wagon from Salt Lake City, its surface had been worn smooth by years of men's elbows. Two tables were occupied besides several other men that sat here and there. Cyrus nodded from behind the bar when Henry walked in.

"You're the man of the hour, Henry," he said. "We just elected you sheriff," at which the men laughed.

"Much obliged, but I'd better wait to hear what the rest of the town says," Henry replied, and they laughed again. He went to a table where J. W. Dillingham, Buzz Caven, and Ned Ray sat, and they invited him to join them. They all had good reputations and Henry liked and respected each of them.

"Glad to see you here all at the same time," Henry said. "I'll need some dependable Union men if I'm elected. The job will pay high in risk but low every other way. How would you men like to help keep the peace?"

They looked at one another and then at Henry.

"I would," Dillingham said. "Don't need much to keep me goin' and I've been lookin' to quit the creek."

"Count me in," Caven said. Ned Ray nodded in agreement.

"Good. We'll find out if we're hired soon enough," Henry said.

Dillingham opened his pocket watch and said, "Votes were taken until noon and it's that now, Henry. I'll go find out how many you got."

Thirty quiet minutes later, all eyes looked to the door as he entered.

"Henry, you got three hundred and seven votes," he said, smiling.

"To what?" Henry said.

"Two hundred and forty seven. Congratulations, Sheriff," Dillingham said, and the men slapped Henry on the back and shook his hand.

"Let's drink to Sheriff Henry Plummer," Cyrus said, and they did.

"Tomorrow you'll have to make a speech when you're sworn in, Henry," Cyrus teased. "What are you going to say?"

"Speech, speech!" Dillingham said, pounding the table with a fist.

Henry stood up and placed his thumbs behind his lapels in the orator's style.

"I appreciate the trust placed in me," he said; "I'm sorry I must leave, but I intend to marry Miss Bryan and bring her back."

"Hooray for Sheriff Henry Plummer!" Cyrus interrupted.

"My deputies are capable and will keep an eye on things until I return. Anyone can understand my position. Thank you for your support."

The men cheered him again, which Henry appreciated. The next day, May 24, 1863, Henry, his chosen few, and the mining judge stood on the steps of the Goodrich Hotel for the swearing-in ceremony. There had been little fanfare about politics among the miners. They had only half the year to find their fortunes so they pretty much ignored the ceremony to a man.

"Do you, Henry Plummer, solemnly swear to uphold the laws of Idaho Territory and the Union of the United States of America?"

"I do," Henry replied, and they shook hands.

"Congratulations, Sheriff Plummer. What will be your first official act?" the judge said, lighting a cigar.

"To swear these men in as my deputies. They're loyal Union men who can be trusted to do their duty."

The judge looked at each of Henry's prospective deputies, puffed his cigar, and said, "I do believe they can hold the fort. Well, the trail from Sun River must be difficult for a woman. I wish you Godspeed there and back."

"Thank you, sir."

"Men, raise your right hands," Henry said. "Do you swear to uphold the laws of Idaho Territory and the Union of the United States of America?" he repeated.

"I do," they replied in unison.

"Congratulations. Here is a list of fines that can be levied for offenses," he said, handing the list to Ned. "I'll start raising money for a jail when I get back, but it wouldn't hurt for you to talk it up. Until then, work with the miner's court if something comes up."

"Good enough, Henry," Caven said. "Keep an eye out for Indians."

Henry simply nodded, mounted his horse, and left town heading north. When he reached the top of the hill he stopped, turned around, and looked back down at the buildings spread along the small valley. They looked like miniature playhouses.

"Well, dear heart," he said, "I'm later than I thought but here I come," and urged his horse on. He had good weather and saw no Indians. Almost a week later, he approached Sun River Farm. He heard someone, probably Joseph, striking a hammer on metal, no doubt in the barn. Electa and Martha had just finished the breakfast dishes as he shut the gate behind him. Everything looked the same as it had the day he left. The hammering had stopped. Strangely, it could have seemed as though he had never left.

"Henry's here!" Joseph shouted and hurried toward the house from the barn.

Those within the house heard the announcement. Martha, James, and Francis looked at one another. Electa gasped and quickly opened the door.

"Oh, he is! He's back!" she cried, and ran outside to greet him.

Chapter Sixteen ~ The Announcement

Henry took off his hat and dropped the reins to his horse as Electa hurried toward him from the house. "Henry!" she cried. Love and relief met in their embrace.

"Darling," he said softly. They gently kissed while James, Martha, and Francis appeared outside the front door.

"I can't tell you how long it has seemed since you left!" she said. "I have so much to tell you, and I want to know all about Bannock City."

"Well, it's not quite a city yet." She closed her eyes and rested her head on his chest, prolonging the moment.

"I have much to tell you," he said, but seeing the trio watching he added, "but first we must see your family. We'll talk later." Smiling, they walked arm in arm to the house.

"Hello, Henry," James said, stepping forward to shake his hand. "You look fit."

"Thank you, sir, the climate has been good for me." Henry offered an honest, straightforward gaze and a sincere smile. "I hope you're well, Mrs.Vail," he said.

"Thank you, yes," she said, but didn't offer her hand. James interrupted the awkward moment.

"Henry, may I present our good friend Francis Thompson," James said.

"Pleased to meet you," Henry said, stepping forward to shake Francis's hand.

"We met Francis on the steamship," James said. "I believe you two have mining in common."

"Oh?" Henry said, genuinely interested.

"You two can talk business later," Electa interrupted, tugging Henry's arm toward the open compound. "Right now, we're going for a walk," she said, smiling.

"Excuse me, ma'am," Henry said, tipping his hat to Martha. "Nice to have met you, Mr. Thompson," he said.

"Call me Francis, Henry."

"We'll see you two later," James said, taking Martha's arm. The three went inside. Away from the house, Henry said, "I'm sure you expected me weeks ago, but I got back as soon as I could."

"What kept you?" Electa asked.

"The election," he teased, smiling.

"What election? And you stop teasing me right now!"

They laughed, happy to be arm in arm, alone and together again.

"My dear, I'm the sheriff of Bannock City!" He grinned, proud of his accomplishment.

"Henry, I'm so proud!"

Side by side they hugged again, followed by another kiss as they walked. "What else have you been up to that I don't know about?" she said.

"Well, I've got several claims that are doing very well, and I bought a house. For after we're married," he said. They stopped walking and faced each other.

"I am so glad to hear that, but I have a confession to make," she said.

Afraid of what she might say next, he felt empty inside, an uncomfortable, new feeling to him, one he didn't like. It reminded him of fear.

"Martha made me promise that I would abide by Francis's advice."

"About what?"

"About whether to marry you or not." She had never seen him look hurt before, and it pained her to know that she had done it. "Francis said that he heard about you on the trail, and that you were an outlaw, and Henry," she said, and her voice failed.

"Go ahead," he said softly. "It's all right." He tilted her chin up gently, until her eyes opened and met his.

"He said you killed Jack."

He sighed, looking at the surrounding hills.

"Is it true? What happened?"

"Electa, I had to." He raised his arm in defense and let it drop to his side in resignation. "He got to drinking too much and turned mean. He wouldn't stop bullying a man, got mad, and drew his gun on us. It's too bad that it happened and I'm sorry it did, but I had no choice. I know you liked him; I did too."

She sighed, accepting his account as true. They began to walk again.

"Well, what's done is done," she said. "It's hard to imagine him gone."

"He wasn't the same man, Electa," he said, shaking his head. "You wouldn't have cared to know him."

Standing in the middle of the compound, she stopped to face him again, and searched his eyes. "I'll take your word for that, Henry Plummer. And you for my husband." Moving closer together, they kissed yet again.

"Darling, how soon can we be married?" Henry said.

"We're waiting for Reverend Reed to arrive. He'll pay James for the year and bring our supplies. We need just about everything. The cows have gone dry and poor Iron was killed by Indians who stole everything he had. All we have to eat is wild meat dressed up with corn meal. Martha is beside herself."

"I'm sorry. I didn't know. But what about people passing through? Can't you buy supplies from them?"

"Someone goes by almost every day, but they're all going to Fort Benton to meet the ship. They need supplies as badly as we do if not worse. I'm glad you're here now."

"Your family isn't very happy to see me, but I didn't come back to please them."

"I told them of your promise the day you left. Martha has been worried."

"She has nothing to worry about because I'll take care of you. After we're married we'll go to Bannock where there are no shortages. Freight wagons come in almost every day from

Salt Lake City. If I had known about your situation I would have brought supplies with me."

"I know you would have," she said, smiling. "Let's go back to the house and tell everyone our plans." Walking hand in hand, the wild daisies looked prettier to Electa than any she could remember. Henry made her cares evaporate like river fog on a bright winter day. "I feel fine, Henry, just like I knew I would. I feel free as a bird, light as a feather, and giddy as a schoolgirl," she said, and they laughed. They reached the house, where Henry opened the door and they went inside.

"Hello, kids," Henry said, greeting the children as they played in a rocking chair.

"Be careful you don't fall out of that chair."

"They entertain themselves playing for hours in that chair, usually until Harvey falls asleep," Electa said. Turning to the trio at the table, she grinned at Henry and said, "I have an announcement to make. As soon as Reverend Reed arrives, Henry and I will be married."

"Electa, I don't understand," Martha began, but James interrupted.

"My dear," he said calmly, "we can rest assured that Electa knows what she is doing. God leads us all down paths that no one else can see. Don't you agree, Electa?"

"Of course. My faith in God and Henry are well founded. Henry is now the sheriff of Bannock City. Everyone knows and respects him," she beamed. "He's also a successful miner and has bought us a house. I'm proud of him for making such a fine start for us."

"Well," Martha said, "I should have more trust in your judgment. I'm just beginning to realize that you're a young woman with a life of your own as well as the fact that you're my little sister. I don't want to keep you from happiness."

"Sit down, you two," James said. "Sorry there's no sugar for coffee, Henry."

"That's fine, thank you," Henry said and waited for Electa to sit down. She sat next to Martha, trying to be close to her while life took her away from the family she had always known. "I'll take care of Electa the best way I can," Henry said. Electa took Martha's hand to reassure her.

"I'm sure you will," Martha said, patting Electa's hand.

"But the people of Bannock depend on me and we can't wait very long."

"How soon do you think you need to be back in Bannock?" Francis said.

"A few weeks should be reasonable," Henry said.

"Iron brought four Indian ponies back during one of the last times he went out," James said. "Maybe you can break them to harness."

"Why? Have you tried?" Henry said.

"No. But I want you to take the government wagon when you leave. I don't want my sister-in-law traveling that far on a horse," he teased.

"Thank you kindly; that's very considerate of you. Sounds like an easy trip now," Henry said, grinning. Electa, thrilled at the thought, squeezed Martha's hand.

~

Before Henry arrived, James and Francis hunted, leaving Joseph to watch the farm. Now three men looked for meat while they waited two weeks for Reverend Reed. The women ground corn meal in a hand mill, which made boring fare indeed. They served johnnycakes, muffins, mush, and Indian pudding to "dress up the meat," as Electa put it.

"Well, your cooking is still delicious, and we don't lack for quantity of food even if variety fails us, Martha," Francis said at breakfast, trying to compliment her.

"Thank you, but I know you're just trying to make me feel better. I am grateful for the deer; it's much better than prairie dog. I didn't care for that," she said, shaking her head. "The meat is tender and sweet. I just don't like the idea of eating dog."

"I prefer prairie chickens," Henry said, and they all laughed. Turning serious he said, "James, I can't wait much longer. It's been two weeks and we haven't heard anything from Fort Benton. I reckon that even with the wagon, it will still take us about a week to get back."

"Henry, we're just going to have to wait," James said. "It's important to us for a minister of our faith to marry Electa. Things will work out fine; you'll see. In the meantime, let's all go on a short excursion to pass the time. It's about thirty miles to the Missouri River. I've heard tell that the waterfalls are a sight to behold. Let's go there to see for ourselves."

"But James, the Indians!" Martha said. "It will be dangerous."

"No more than our last picnic. We didn't see any then," James said, smiling and winking at Henry. "From what I've heard, the waterfalls will be worth the trouble. We'll leave notice for the Reverend to wait here in case he arrives. Let's just pack the wagon and go," he said, pointing toward the door to show his determination.

"Well, all right," Martha shrugged. "Come, dear, let's get to work." She got up from the table followed by Electa, who smiled at Henry while leaving.

"We'd better pack plenty of food," Electa said. "An adventure like this is going to make all of these men hungry."

Chapter Seventeen ~ Diversion, Danger, and a Priest

"All right, gentlemen," Martha said to James and Francis in the kitchen. "Would you carry this box and these baskets of food to the wagon, please?"

Outside, Henry waited beside the wagon. When Electa came out, he helped her up to her seat. After mounting his horse he said, "Reminds me of another picnic."

"Yes, but there will be no horse racing today," Electa said with a somber look.

"Yes, ma'am," Henry acknowledged. Stung by her rebuke, he tipped his hat. He thought he had better hide his tongue for awhile.

They left the farm and headed due east. Henry rode beside Electa as before. She noticed that he still rode as one with his horse, which led her thoughts back to the race and Jack. Strangely, it seemed like so long ago, yet also like just yesterday. But now Jack didn't ride behind them. He couldn't have done anything about her choosing Henry, and she couldn't do anything about Jack's decisions or blame Henry for them. But Jack's end still saddened her. Her mood brightened somewhat along the way while watching Henry ride and as she and Martha sang to the children. Late in the day they came upon a ravine.

"We'll camp here for the night," James announced. "We're not likely to be spotted down here. We'll reach the falls tomorrow about midmorning and won't stay very long. We needed to get away, but it's also important to get back."

The next morning they started early and saw no Indians. They could hear the roar of the falls long before they approached the edge of the river, where James finally reined the team up under cottonwood trees. The family got out and stretched their legs. No one said very much. Henry and Electa held hands as they stood at the river's edge and watched the natural wonder.

The tremendous noise and incredible view impressed them all. The continuously massive, steady surge poured over the huge underwater cliff and dropped down into a crashing white heap before flowing on.

"Isn't that an amazing sight!" exclaimed Martha. "Look at the waterfalls, children. It's a sight none of us will probably ever forget."

"Mercy!" Electa said. "How big are they, James? How high, and how far across?"

"It's hard to guess, but I would say they're at least eighty feet tall and probably three hundred feet across. Would you agree, Francis?"

"I wouldn't have any better guess," Francis said. "What an astonishing sight. Needless to say, if Captain Lewis's and Clark's canoes couldn't navigate them, no steamship ever could."

"Imagine," Electa said, "the Corps of Discovery was here just sixty years ago!"

A large flat plateau rose to the south, the only high country in sight, but all eyes remained transfixed on the falls. James had been right. They had needed such a diversion to get their minds off their situation. The waterfall's beauty and the soothing, rhythmic sound of the pounding water seemed to refresh everyone.

"I wish we had such a breathtaking sight by Sun River Farm," Electa said.

"I expect God knew best where to put waterfalls," Martha said.

"And I expect we'd better be getting back," James said. "I don't want to leave the farm too long. The less we're away, the better."

After just a short time they started back. Martha gave corn dodgers to everyone on the way since James didn't want to stop for dinner. By the time they came in sight of the farm, the sun had begun to send yellow streaks through low clouds. Henry and

Francis discussed mining while riding out in front of the wagon. Suddenly, Henry reined his horse and quickly rode back to the wagon. James reined the horses up.

"James," Henry said, touching his hat brim for the women, "the farm is surrounded by Indian ponies. Sorry to have to alarm you, ladies. What do you want to do, James?"

"Take James and Joseph closer, and carry your rifles. If they're Blackfeet, come back. If they're Flatheads, tell them that we want our home back, and right now."

Henry waved for Joseph to come up from the rear and saw fear in Electa's eyes. He gave her a grin and a nod that told her everything would be all right. When Joseph reached them, the three men spurred their horses toward the farm. James looked around nervously, suddenly realizing that the wagon could be attacked while the men were gone. Martha noticed. "How long do you think they'll be gone, dear?" she said.

"Just a few minutes. I'm sure it's nothing serious. At least there's no smoke," he said, trying to reassure her.

Indians outside the perimeter of the compound saw the men approaching and rode to the front gate, yelling warning cries.

The three men rode around the compound and cut off the escape of a half dozen Indians riding out of the gate on horseback. All wore braids; some had leather leggings, others only breechcloths. Henry fired a shot in the air.

"Stop right there!" he called out.

"Food!" one of them said. "We want food!"

"There's none to spare. You stay put. Joseph, go get James." The Indians sat quietly, seemingly embarrassed at getting caught. By the time the wagon got there James was a welcome enough sight, although the sight of that many braves frightened his family. He reined up the wagon and stood up to address the trespassers.

"The Flatheads are not to come here when we're gone," James said. "This is our property. You have no right to be here.

If you do this again I'll have to punish you. Now go and come back when you're ready to grow many plants that will feed you."

The three men remained mounted outside the compound until James took the wagon safely inside and the Indians retreated to the top of the hill. Once inside the house, Henry again brought up the wedding while the ladies put things away.

"James, time is up. I'm going to ride to Fort Benton to find out about the ship."

"I see. Well, you'd better take Joseph along. Two are safer than one," he said, looking at Electa.

"We'll leave at daybreak," Henry said.

~

Three days later the two tired men rode back into the compound. James heard the horses and went outside to meet them. He nodded a greeting.

"You two look trail-worn and weary. What's the word from Fort Benton?"

"The *Shreveport* can't get upriver," Henry said. "Not enough water."

"I see. I'd better tell the women," James said, and he went back inside.

"I'll take care of your horse, Henry," Joseph said and led them toward the barn.

"Much obliged," Henry said. Electa met him at the door of the house.

"Hello, darling," he said, and they kissed before holding hands and going inside.

"James told us about the ship," she said. James and Martha sat at the table, resigned looks on their faces. Electa said what they were all thinking. "I don't see any alternative but to send for the priest at the mission. It's not fair to us to drag this on any further."

"You're right, of course," James said. "I'll send Joseph as soon as he's rested."

Electa and Henry smiled at one another. "At long last, our wedding," Henry said.

"At long last," she repeated.

Joseph rode to the mission that afternoon. When he arrived, he found the Catholic priest toiling in his small fenced garden under the hot sun. The church stood nearby, built longer to the rear than wide, with a small room in the back that served as the priest's living quarters. The building had a two-story tower over the entryway crowned by a wooden cross. The priest leaned on his rake, smiled, and took off his round-brimmed black hat as Joseph approached.

"Welcome," he said. He wiped his brow and replaced his hat. "I'm Father Joseph Minatre. Please get down and come in."

"Thank you, no," Joseph said. "I need to get back right away. They'll be wanting to know your answer."

"To where must you return so soon?"

"Sun River Farm. It's not too far from here."

"And you need my answer about what?"

"Henry's the sheriff at Bannock City, and Electa lives at the farm. They need to know whether you'll marry them or not. We've been waiting for a preacher to come through Fort Benton but the water's too shallow."

"Of course I will marry them. But I am saddened to hear that they would rather have a Protestant ceremony," he smiled, teasing Joseph.

"You know how it is, Reverend. Each to their own," Joseph said. "Once it's done I guess it won't matter much who did it."

"Of course you are right. I will come tomorrow if you will tell me how to get there." Joseph did so and bid him farewell.

Upon his return, everyone met Joseph outside the house. "He'll be here early tomorrow, probably for breakfast," he said.

"How wonderful!" Electa said, clasping her hands. She and Martha hugged.

"That is good news," James agreed. Since no supplies or money were coming in the foreseeable future, he didn't mind having a little less responsibility. Not that he wasn't happy for them, but the practical side of the situation didn't escape him either.

"Dear, I'm so happy for you both," Martha said.

"We'll be married as soon as he arrives," Henry said, smiling at Electa.

"Congratulations to both of you," Francis said, shaking Henry's hand.

Joseph tipped his hat before leaving. "I wish you both the best," he said. "We'll sure miss you."

"Thank you," Electa said. "We'll miss everyone here, too. But perhaps we'll see each other before too long. You'll all be welcome at our home in Bannock."

"If we don't get supplies soon we may all have to go to Bannock," James said. "We can't continue like this for very long."

"Bannock can always use new citizens," Henry said. "It's growing, and supplies arrive from Salt Lake City every week."

"I almost forget how to cook with anything besides corn meal," Martha said.

"Well, we haven't gone hungry," Electa said. "The good Lord has provided. No one can deny that."

"When do you plan to leave for Bannock, Henry?" James said.

"Right after breakfast," he said, grinning at Electa.

They all had much to do before Father Minatre arrived the next morning. James had Joseph prepare the government wagon for the trip. Martha and Electa got the wedding dress ready and prepared a buffalo hump Francis brought home for the wedding breakfast. Electa packed practically all of her things. On her last evening at Sun River Farm, she again wrote Victoria.

Dear Victoria,   June 19, 1863

I hope this finds you fair and well, as we are here. How can I express my joy? I am to marry Henry Plummer tomorrow morning! Martha has finally accepted the fact. I am proud that he is a gold miner and the sheriff of Bannock City. I have no idea what our life will be like in such a place as I have never been, but no matter. Our Lord will see me through. I will gladly face a new place as long as Henry is beside me. Unfortunately we are still without supplies here since no ship can navigate the low river. Henry and I will travel by wagon, which he says will take a week. I can't imagine a more exciting honeymoon! A week together in the wilderness with Indians about on the way to a new life in a new town! We have had no news of the war, but Henry says that Union gold must not reach rebel hands in the south. I will post this as soon as possible.

Devotedly, Electa.

Chapter Eighteen ~ The Wedding

As Joseph had predicted, Father Minatre arrived before breakfast. Joseph opened the gate for him while James waited at the door of the house as their guest approached. "Greetings in the name of our Lord," the priest said. "I am Father Minatre."

"Welcome," James replied. "Thank you for coming, Father. Please come in and meet everyone." The priest entered while taking off his hat, and James paused in the doorway for a moment. "Joseph, please ask Henry to come to the house," he called.

Henry had just finished getting ready at the cabin. On his wedding day he wore a blue suit foxed with buckskin on the collar, sleeve ends, and pockets over a checked cotton shirt and blue tie.

"Don't you look like the cat who got the bird," Joseph said. "Nervous?"

"You want to bet against it?" Henry said, which made Joseph laugh. "You don't look too bad yourself. I appreciate you being my best man."

"Proud to do it. Thanks for asking me," Joseph said. He wore a gray flannel shirt and gray pants divided by a colorful red and white sash. His pants were foxed with buckskin on the pockets as well. For the occasion, he showed off a pair of Blackfoot moccasins he had traded for.

Introductions were made with the priest while Henry and Joseph walked to the house. When they arrived they found Electa waiting at the door. She wore a modest brown calico dress.

"Morning, ma'am," Joseph said. "Don't you look fine on your wedding day. I don't expect you're waiting for me," he teased, making Henry chuckle.

"Good morning, darling," Electa said, squeezing Henry's hand as she led him inside. "Henry, I'd like you to meet Father Minatre from the mission."

"How do you do, sir," Henry said, and they shook hands, looking at each other squarely in the eye.

"How do you do, young man. You have an honest handshake. And I don't trust a man who won't look a priest in the eye," he smiled, his eyes twinkling. "It's said that the eyes are the windows to the soul, and I like what I see in your eyes, young man. Thank you for asking me to perform your marriage ceremony. I deem it both an honor and a privilege."

"You're welcome. Thank you for coming. We don't know what we would have done, otherwise."

"God always makes a way, my son."

"Yes, I've found that to be so," Henry said, looking at Electa.

"Will the marriage take place before or after breakfast?" Father Minatre said, looking at Martha.

"If it's all the same to you, before," Henry said. "Just as soon as we can."

"Well, then, let's all gather together over here in the parlor," the priest said, holding his arm out. "My dear, you don't have a bridesmaid. Mr. Thompson, perhaps you could serve in that capacity?"

"Of course. Your wish is my command," Francis replied. He was dressed in moleskin pants, a brown shirt, black coat, vest, and buffalo hide shoes he had acquired on his western travels.

The priest centered himself in the room and waited for everyone to take their places. Electa and Henry stood before him, smiling. She noticed how the lamplight glow caught the red in Henry's hair. As acting bridesmaid, Francis stood off to Electa's side while Joseph, the best man, stood opposite on Henry's side. The priest prayed in Latin and made the sign of the cross on himself as well as over the couple before proceeding.

"Dearly beloved, we are gathered together in this humble home to witness the marriage ceremony of Mr. Henry Plummer and Miss Electa Bryan," he began. He carried on much longer than Henry thought he should have, talking about such things as marriage, the home the young couple was about to establish, and the great need for churches in towns such as Bannock. Henry didn't understand what that had to do with much, but it was the priest's chance to talk, and talk he did, for a good long time. Finally, about the time Martha began to worry about the buffalo hump on the stove, the good Father brought the ceremony-sermon to a close.

"Electa, do you take this man to be your lawfully wedded husband, to have and to hold, to honor and obey, from this day forward?"

"I do," she said, smiling at Henry.

"Henry, do you take this woman to be your lawfully wedded wife, to have and to hold, to love and to cherish, from this day forward?"

"I do," he said, returning her smile.

"Then by the power vested in me by the holy church, I pronounce you husband and wife. Henry, you may kiss your bride."

Henry gently pulled Electa close. They had eyes only for each other as he tenderly kissed her in the pale yellow light. When she stepped back, the priest introduced them to the small audience.

"Ladies and gentlemen, I present Mr. and Mrs. Henry Plummer."

Everyone applauded while Martha approached Electa. "My dear, you look somehow different than before the wedding," she said, holding her hands. "Older, more mature."

"I doubt that," Electa said. "It's the way you see me that's different. How do you see Henry now that we're married?"

Martha looked at him, sighed, and smiled. "As the handsome, responsible young man I know we'll all be very proud of."

"That's enough sentiment for now," James said. "These people want to start traveling, so we'd better eat so they can." As they walked to the table he added, "Thank you, Reverend, that was quite a ceremony."

"Neither my sermons nor my ceremonies are known to be short and sweet. But some have said that I am 'long and pompous,' the priest said, at which everyone laughed.

Martha and Electa hugged again before stepping into the kitchen to serve breakfast. James took care of the children while everyone else sat down to a plain but delicious breakfast of buffalo hump and cornmeal bread.

"Dear, I hate to insist, but we have a long wagon ride ahead of us," Henry said when they had finished eating.

"Yes, you're right," Electa said. "But first I need to help Martha with the dishes one more time."

"Nonsense," Martha said. "Henry is right; you've got a long trip ahead of you."

"Well, all right," Electa said, "if you insist. Come here, you two, and give me one more hug and kiss before I go," she said to Mary and Harvey. "Lord knows when I'll see you again."

"I don't think it will be too long," Henry said. "You folks are welcome to come when you can."

"Thank you, we appreciate that," James said. "We'd better get the rest of Electa's things in the wagon. Maybe she'll be ready by then," he teased.

Joseph had hitched James's gift of four Indian ponies to the wagon and driven the team up to the house. They finished packing the wagon and tied Henry's horse behind it.

"If it wasn't your honeymoon, I'd ask if Joseph could ride along. Safety in numbers, you know," James said.

"Much obliged, but I've got two rifles besides handguns. I can handle any trouble and don't expect any. The most Indians will do at night is steal horses, and I'll hobble and tie them to the wagon. I'm a light sleeper anyway, so don't fret about it."

Martha and Electa came outside. Their puffy red eyes said they'd been crying.

"I knew this would be hard," Henry said. "A new start means change and not all of them good."

"You're beginning a new life together, the both of you," James said. "But the Lord is with you, and Electa is up to anything that might come along."

"I hope you're right," Henry said. "Unless you get some supplies pretty quick, you'll have to join us in Bannock."

"Joseph and Francis have been talking about starting a store there. But first they'll have to get a few wagonloads of supplies for a start. They're going to see about it tomorrow."

"That's it then," Henry said, holding out his hand. James took it and smiled. As Henry helped Electa up into the wagon, Father Minatre, Francis, James, Martha, Harvey, Mary, and Joseph all smiled their well-wishes. Electa began to cry again as Henry climbed up, taking the reins in hand.

"I never knew I could be so happy and so sad at the same time," Electa said.

"We feel the same way," Francis said.

There was nothing left but for Henry to slap the reins and drive through the gate.

Chapter Nineteen ~ Wilderness Honeymoon

Waving goodbye, Electa couldn't help but smile through her tears. They rode through the gate sitting together tall and proud, arm in arm, happy, and finally married. Joseph stood at the open gate and watched the four Indian ponies, the couple in the wagon, and then Henry's horse pass by. He wished that he could have tagged along to keep watch for them, but couldn't blame them for wanting their privacy. Finally he closed the gate and walked forlornly to the bunkhouse. He would miss both of them and felt alone, even though he and Francis would now share the little cabin. Martha stood by the house sobbing and quivering, overwhelmed by tremendous feelings of loss that washed over her spirit in a wave of grief. James supported her with an arm around her waist.

"Come, dear," he said gently, "let's go back inside. They'll be fine. All we can do now is pray for them." Francis and the children followed them in while James helped Martha to the table.

"I feel I shall never see my dear sister again," she sobbed, her hands shaking.

"I'm sure the good Lord will reunite two kindred spirits such as yours," Francis said in an effort to encourage her.

"Oh, with all my heart I hope you are right. I couldn't bear otherwise," she said.

Electa began to turn around for one last look but Henry gently took her arm.

"It will help if you don't look back," he said.

"Thank you," she said. "Where do you think we'll stop for the night?"

"The Dearborn River," he said, surprised at her question. "I picked out a pretty little spot on the way up. I'll cut some pine branches for our bed. Nothing smells better when you're sleeping outside."

She blushed at that.

"Of course, we'll be under the wagon," he said.

"Under the wagon?"

"That's right, on a buffalo robe. The wagon will keep the morning dew off. We'll hang blankets around the sides so the horses don't watch us on our wedding night," he teased.

"Henry!" she said, slapping his shoulder, and they laughed.

When the sun rose highest in the big sky, they stopped for lunch long enough to eat deer meat sandwiches and stretch their legs.

"What are you grinning about?" she said.

"How fun it is to take you through country you've never seen before."

"I did it week after week on the Missouri," she said matter-of-factly.

"Yes, but I didn't take you on that trip," he said, which reminded her of her family, and he knew it. She tried to hide it, but he saw her wipe a tear away. Angry with himself, he promised himself it wouldn't happen again.

"Do you think we'll see anyone on the way?" she said.

"Probably not. We'll go south past Crown Butte and stay in the valleys when we can. But we'll have to cross two mountain passes, and the first one is pretty high. You'll see flowers there you've never seen before," he said, trying to cheer her up. "When we get south far enough, we'll turn west before the hills climb back into the high mountains."

"Is that where Bannock is?" she asked.

He smiled. "No, not quite. We'll cut west, climb up and over a short, easy divide, down into a little valley, and that's where Bannock is."

At that, she squeezed his arm, excited at the thought of seeing her new home for the first time. For the rest of the day he guided the lively paint ponies around hills that sat just north of the Dearborn River as it meandered southwest to the Missouri.

"Woah, you renegades," Henry said, pulling on the reins. They had reached the grassy meadow he had picked out beside the Dearborn. He helped her down from the wagon and was rewarded with a kiss.

"You were right. It is pretty here," she said, smiling. "If you'll start a fire, I'll get supper ready."

"Sounds fair to me, after I hobble the horses," he said, returning her smile.

He took care of the horses and struck a match within a circle of stones under tinder and sticks. While she prepared the food, he spread a blanket by the river for them to sit on away from the smoke of the fire. It seemed to Electa as though they sat on a magic carpet floating on a sea of green grass decorated with white sweet clover blossoms and black-eyed Susans. They watched the water slip by and shared bread, smoked fish, and fresh, clear water from the Dearborn during their first evening together as a married couple.

"It reminds me of the Missouri slipping by the *Emilie*," she said, laying back and cradling her head in her arms.

"I'm glad you came," he said softly, and they kissed.

"I am too. What are the people like in Bannock?"

"Like people anywhere else, I guess."

"Well, then," she said, "what are the women like?"

"A mystery, mostly," he said, teasing her, and laughed. "Like any women, I guess. Why?"

"I was just thinking how different life is going to be from now on. If I'll have friends."

"You'll have me," he said, tickling her nose with a flower.

"I know that," she said, taking it from him while giving him a peck of a kiss. "I mean women friends."

"Sure enough, if you want them. Being sheriff is going to take most of my time. Running a new gold town isn't easy. And I've been gone longer than I thought. Who knows what's happened since I left."

"God knows," she said. The simple profound fact almost bore repeating, but he didn't.

"But He's not going to tell me," he said. "It's my job to get there and to find out."

"Of course it is," she said, smiling. "You know, it will soon be dark."

A cool breeze came across the water. The fire popped, reminding him that it needed to be fed. He looked at her and smiled. He wanted to always remember her with the last sun glistening through her hair, outlined against the hills and sky behind her. Yes, he would always remember.

"I can take a hint," he said, getting up to feed the fire. "I'll cut some pine boughs if you'll unpack the sheets and blankets. Is it a deal?"

She smiled as she got up and said, "It's a deal."

Electa got the sheets and waited. She looked up into the darkening sky where the stars had begun to appear. In a short while Henry returned. He retrieved a buffalo robe and climbed underneath the wagon to arrange the boughs.

"You're right," she said. "The fresh boughs smell wonderful."

He unrolled the large furry robe over the aromatic mattress he had fashioned and stood up to admire his handiwork. He tried to fit the circular hide squarely under the rectangular wagon, but its excessive bulk spilled out between the wheels. "I'd better light a lamp before we do anything else," he said.

Electa tried to see across the river but darkness had materialized. The almost silently moving water appeared to be black. Together, the newlyweds hung sheets over the wheels and around the outside of the wagon.

"If we tuck them in tightly next to your trunks and bags, they should stay even if a wind comes up," he said, looking around. "There's no sign of rain so I think we'll be all right."

She knelt at the back of the wagon so she could enter the newly fashioned shelter.

"Here, I'll hold the door open for you," he teased, pulling back a sheet. "And I'll hold the lamp so you can get the blankets situated. But watch your head unless you want a headache."

"I never want a headache, and especially not on my wedding night," she said, which made him glad for the darkness as he smiled. She crawled underneath the wagon, pulling the blankets in after her. "The robe is so soft!" she said. "We'll sleep like babies with full tummies."

"It's been awhile since we've been babies," he said, making her grin.

He kneeled to watch as she fashioned one blanket to serve as their pillow. It took only a minute to straighten another and put the finishing touches on their bed.

"We've got another long ride tomorrow," she said and leaned toward him to blow the lamp out.

Chapter Twenty ~ Bad News upon Arrival

Of course, the wilderness newlyweds learned much more about each other on the trail. She treasured every day as an adventure. Electa found Henry to be quieter than she had thought, but reckoned that to natural shyness about being with a new wife, not to mention his new responsibilities as sheriff. But in between the quiet times Henry tried to keep her mind off Sun River Farm in general and Martha in particular.

"Yes, ma'am, my life is rising to a huckleberry above a persimmon," Henry said, grinning and teasing her. "I'm a big bug with the prettiest wife in a new town."

"I suppose that makes me a bug too," Electa teased back.

Bumping along hour after hour reminded her of the trip from Fort Benton to Sun River Farm. She had fairly dreaded facing an entire week of the same. How sad, she thought, that the disappointing place had not turned out as sunny as its name. But being with Henry made all the difference. Since they spent practically every hour together, she wondered whether they would tire of each other's company before they even reached Bannock. Instead, it seemed that the days dashed by too quickly. She'd not seen such beautiful country, and their meals seemed an exploration compared to the simple fare at the farm.

Along the way Henry shot rabbits, grouse, and a turkey. She showed him, as Iron had taught her, how to find wild onions and roots, which deliciously flavored the meat of two sage hens he killed by throwing rocks. And as enjoyable as the scenery, meals, and the company were, Electa thought the nights even better. Lying next to Henry felt even more comfortable and natural than she had ever dreamed. On the day Henry announced they would arrive, the late June sun warmed their backs as the lone wagon climbed into the foothills that cradled Bannock.

"Today I'll see where you've been keeping yourself," she said, teasing again.

"That's right," he said. "Everyone allows I'm the biggest toad in the puddle."

"Oh, Henry!" she said, laughing. "I know you, and you could never believe such balderdash. Big bugs and toads indeed."

"Electa," Henry said. She looked at him questioningly, waiting for him to continue. "Bannock is a rough town. You won't be able to go out alone. Main Street isn't safe for decent women. I should have told you before, but I didn't think it would make any difference."

"Of course it doesn't. I'll be fine at home and you'll be with me when I'm out."

"I'll have to be or you won't be safe." He paused and said, "That's not all."

"What else? What's bothering you?" she asked, smiling to reassure him.

"There's no church or school," he said, expressionless. "And there's no telling how much I'll be gone working. I fear frontier life will be even harder for you than it has been."

"Oh," she said. "I see." She suddenly realized that the mere presence of people didn't promise civilization or, it seemed, freedom from isolation. The contentment she sought appeared to be escaping her grasp before she could capture a thimble full of it.

"What *does* it have?" she wanted to know.

"When I left, two hotels, two smiths, two stables, let's see, a grocery, two butchers, a brewery, and four saloons, give or take," he said in an attempt to tease her.

"Give or take what?" she asked, refusing the tease and pressing him.

"Nothing," he said, giving up the attempt. "There's only four."

"Only four saloons. We should thank heaven for even small favors," she said, teasing him now, which made them both laugh.

"At first a row of houses was built on the south side of the creek, but shanties are scattered all over now. Our place isn't far behind Main Street, which is rough business, as I said. It's rambunctious over there, so you'll have to stay away." She nodded her understanding and wondered about the place.

The broken gray-green sagebrush cracked under the horse's hooves and wagon wheels. About mid-morning they came to a wide trail evidently made by scores of wagon and horse tracks.

"A road. A new scar on the face of creation," Electa said.

"Can't tell if they were headed east or west," Henry said. "A lot of folks have either been going to Bannock or" he paused, "leaving. Wonder why. Probably gold. We'll just follow this road as long as it takes us to home."

When the sun crowned the sky, they stopped to eat and rest the horses on the pine-studded crest of what seemed to Electa to be a mountain. During the slow gradual climb she couldn't see that it was a relatively flat ridge-top running north and south. Except for the fragrant pines, they could have seen fifty miles in any direction. Behind them, the grand, graceful land fell gently eastward to a river twenty miles away, eventually rising into hills, building yet again into mountains. To the west, another wall of white-topped mountains sat like some great, long, white backbone breaking the endlessly deep blue sky. Between them and the backbone lay an immense bowl of land filled with buffalo grass and sagebrush. Henry reined the ponies up so they could rest and cool off in the shade of some tall pines.

"We'll be in town before supper whether we mosey or let her rip," Henry said.

"I don't know if I'm more nervous or excited," Electa said.

"There's nothing to be nerved up about a one-horse town. I reckon they've seen a wagon pull in before."

"Yes, but they've not seen their sheriff's new wife before."

"No, but when they do, they'll take notice," he said, making her blush.

"I know. That's why I'm so nervous," she said.

Henry tried to ease her apprehension with light talk. After a while they left the picnic spot and wound further west down a long gradual slope. A few hours later he stopped the wagon. Below them and a half-mile away, a group of buildings sat in a narrow valley.

"Down there is Bannock City," Henry said, nodding toward the site. To Electa, the buildings looked strangely out of place after a week in the wilderness.

"There are no trees near the town," she said.

"They've been used for cabins and to shore up flea pits in the hills. Some miners don't take time to build. They just hollow out a place in the dirt to sleep."

"And those Indian tents off a ways. There must be a dozen of them."

"Shoshoni," Henry said. "They hunt a little and drink as much as possible."

He snapped the reins, rousing the ponies to move on down the hill. The sagebrush continued to crackle under the wheels. After a short while they could see men digging and moving, working as they searched for rich dirt in the large hill across the canyon. Others, appearing as ants, worked the creek that ran through the middle of town. The Main Street ran the same direction as the valley. A half-hour later they reached the valley floor and entered the east end of town. As they approached, Electa noticed that the front of most Main Street buildings had a flat, high front to them, making them appear taller from the front than they really were.

"Why did they put such fronts on the buildings? I've never seen anything like it."

"Oh, it lets folks feel like they're in a big city, I suspicion," Henry said, grinning.

"Hello, Sheriff! Welcome back!" Folks called out, waving and smiling from doorways and wooden sidewalks. He nodded and gave his easy smile back. Several men worked at loading a wagon at the north side of the street. He noticed empty buildings here and there with locked doors. "Something's not right," he said.

"What's wrong?" Electa said. "They're certainly friendly."

"Lots of folks have gone somewhere on that new road," he said, reining up as a rough looking man approached their wagon. "Hello, Ned," Henry said. "Meet my bride, Electa; Electa, meet Ned Ray, one of my deputies."

"Hello, ma'am. Pleased to meet you," Ned said, lifting his hat in respect.

"How do you do," Electa said, smiling. He hadn't shaved in a week and needed a clean change of clothes, but he was polite and friendly.

"Glad you got back with your Missus, Henry."

"Where is everyone, Ned? Half the town is gone."

"A week after you left, Bill Fairweather and some boys made a big strike east of here. Things have been jumping like hoppers ever since."

Henry nodded. "Do tell. Folks have been jumping out of here, I reckon," he said.

"Dillingham is cold as a wagon tire, Henry."

Henry looked at him sharply with no surprise evident in his expression. "How?" he said. Electa took his arm to remind him that she was there. She had no desire to here the how of it. She could feel the attention of Henry's responsibilities pulling him away from her, and she didn't care for it.

"Shot in a groggery by the new diggings. Buck, Haze, and Charlie Forbes were charged, but Charlie was let go. A bunch of women showed up when Buck and Haze were about to be hung and got the crowd to feeling pitiful about it, so they let them go."

"So no one paid for killing poor Dillingham," Henry said.

"Sorry, Henry," Ned said. "Nothing much I could do about it."

Henry just nodded his understanding. "Meet me at Chrisman's store in the morning," he said, to which Ned nodded. Henry slapped the horses with the reins while Ned touched his hat brim for Electa. She politely smiled as the wagon pulled away.

"I'm sorry about Mr. Dillingham, Henry," she said.

"He was a good man and will be sorely missed. I doubt his caliber can be replaced, which, I reckon, means I'll be short-handed."

So Henry warned her, in his kind way, that it would be necessary for him to be gone much of the time. Electa's heart sank within her. She hadn't even seen her new home yet and already felt isolated. She thought it strange how despair and loneliness could surface just as quickly as hope and companionship.

Chapter Twenty One ~ The Ultimatum

Electa felt Henry's deep sadness over the murder of Dillingham and wanted to encourage him. "I know you'll do a fine job for us," she said. "I want you to know I'll do my best as well."

He knew that she had tried to help him in her own way, so he gave her a slight grin and said, "Here's our palace," as he reined the ponies up in front of a small, simple cabin. Henry looked at the sky before getting down. "We've got about an hour of light left," he said.

"Then we'd better get busy," she said.

"I'll have to make sure no varmints have made themselves to home before you go in," he said and jumped down from the wagon. He helped her down and gently held her arm while escorting her the short distance to the door. He pushed it open, revealing the dark interior and stepped inside. Electa waited anxiously, looking around at the unfamiliar buildings and strangers here and there. After a few moments he reappeared at the door.

"Let me help you," he said. Sweeping her up in a romantic gesture, he carried her over the rough-cut wooden threshold into their new home before setting her back down. "It only has a dirt floor, but I'll peg some hides down," he said.

"That would be nice," she replied, taking a deep breath. "But the wood smells wonderful."

"The place can't be but a year old," he said. "It should do for a time." He took her in his arms, and they kissed in the semidarkness of the empty place.

"Remember, the sun is setting," she said softly. "If you want supper you'll have to unload the wagon and fetch supplies from the store."

"Well, you know I want supper," he said, letting her go.

She made a fire in the stove while he unloaded the wagon.

"What do you need from town before I unhitch the team?" he said, setting down an armload of blankets.

"Here," she said, handing him a piece of paper.

He took it and read aloud, "Soap, washtub, salt, pepper, meat, coffee, tea, syrup, potatoes, sugar, canned fruit, crackers; this is going to take awhile."

"Then you should leave and hurry," she teased.

Knowing she should get busy, she stood in the door while he turned the team around in the street. She waved, then watched him turn the wagon onto Main Street. Leaving the door open to air out the place as well as for the remaining light, she lit some candles and lard-oil lamps before turning to her work knowing that she faced it alone. She and Martha used to get so much done together. She paused at the table to pray.

"Father, thank You for a safe journey, for answering my prayers, and for a new life with Henry. Please watch over Martha, James, the children, Francis, and Joseph at the farm. Father, I'm afraid this is a dangerous place, so please keep Henry safe. Amen."

During the first two weeks in Bannock, Henry was gone from home for a total of ten days. He had found the new gold strike in Alder Gulch, as they called it, so he would know where to go if there was any trouble, which, as he said, was likely.

"They're spread up and down that gulch for ten miles and more," Henry said at supper. "That dig has more going on than Bannock ever will. But we're not moving now. The freighters and stage line will have to pass through here on the way to Salt Lake anyway, and besides, we just got here."

"You don't have time to build us a cabin there, either," Electa said. She gathered what few dishes there were, simple tin plates and cups. "You hardly have time to come home occasionally. Between mining your own claims, riding all over the territory, and making sure everyone within a hundred miles behaves, your wife hasn't seen much of you so far."

She didn't mean to complain, but she had never spent so much time alone in her entire life. True to his word, Henry wouldn't let her go to Main Street for any reason. "It just wasn't done by decent women, and it wasn't safe," he had said. She was afraid to ask what kind of indecent women frequented the town. And she had to admit that the occasional gunshots unnerved her somewhat.

"The claims will be our fortune and future," Henry said. "I've got to make sure my men stay on, and work the mines myself besides, or I'll be claim-jumped. I won't allow that. And the strike at Alder Gulch has spread out my sheriffing responsibilities."

Electa wanted to say that he had responsibilities at home that were at least as important as a few thousand strangers, but held her tongue. She wanted him to think of his home as a peaceful place so he would come back when he could and not stay away because of anything she said.

"Will you take me to Chrisman's store before you have to leave again?" she asked. She didn't know why she said it, or if she did, she wouldn't admit it, even to herself. She already knew his answer.

"No, it's not safe yet. There are too many rowdies firing their pistols without any regard for women and children," he said. "Maybe after I build a jail, they'll think twice. But I will escort you to a dance."

"A dance?" she repeated softly. "I've never been to one and don't believe I'd care to go, thank you." She stood to wash the dishes.

"But you've not met anyone since we got here," he said.

"Henry, as far as I know there isn't anyone here worth knowing besides you, and you've been gone most of the time. My friends have always been in the church and school, and there isn't either one here. Now you want me to go to a dance, something I know nothing about and have no desire to do."

That surprised him. He knew she missed Martha and thought she'd be pleased about the prospect of getting out and meeting some other women. He assumed that she would jump at the chance, but instead she had jumped away from it. Maybe she didn't understand that he would be obliged to go. He turned toward her and straddled the bench he sat on.

"Well, we've not talked about it, but I thought you knew how. I can teach you. It's not until Friday a week, and it won't be a riotous frolic. Besides, lots of folks expect to meet you there."

"Thank you," she said, "but I'm afraid not. I don't set store in any such thing."

"Well, I reckon I'll have to go anyway," he said, leaning back against the wall. "Don't know what I'll say about you, though."

"Henry Plummer, don't you go making any excuses for me," she said firmly, pausing while washing the dishes. "I'd rather have the reputation as a churchgoing lady even if there isn't a church to go to. Maybe you wouldn't need a jail if you built a church instead."

He chuckled, trying to lighten the conversation. "Well, you might be right about that, but I'd be laughed out of the territory if I built a church instead of minding my business. You know I'm no preacher."

"No, you're not, and that's fine. And I don't attend dances, and that will have to be fine with you. Besides, I couldn't bear for Martha to catch wind of such a thing."

He reckoned that it was about time to change the subject. "It seems that Horan and Keeley have had a difficulty," he said, sipping his coffee.

"About what?" Electa said, glad for the shift. "Aren't they partners?"

"They were. Horan wants to sell out. He claimed Keeley tried to cheat him, so it's all going to a sheriff's sale."

"When will you hold that?"

"Tomorrow," Henry said.

The next day, Horan went to Keeley's and coolly shot him dead. Most everyone in Bannock heard the gunshot. Quickly captured, Horan had tried to escape but never reached the horse he had readied. He was tried and found guilty before a miner's court. The judge ordered Henry to build a gallows and to "hang him by the neck until dead." Henry thought better than to go home before the revolting deed had been done. He knew Electa would want him to have none of it. After Henry and his deputies had built the gallows and Horan had been hanged, several deputies tied him to a horse to be taken up on the hill to be buried. That evening, Henry told her about it.

"How horrible!" she said. "How could you have done such an awful thing!"

"It's unpleasant, but has to be done," Henry said. "I'm proud to have done my duty. We can't abide cold-blooded murder. Even the Good Book condemns that."

"You're right, of course," Electa said. "But I still can't stand the very thought of it. If you must execute any more men, please keep me in the dark about it."

He thought it best to change the subject, never to be brought up again.

"Oh, and I hope to hear from the Freemasons soon," Henry said. Covering his mouth with his napkin, he coughed hard, which turned his face red.

"You're not getting enough rest the way it is," she said. "Isn't it enough to belong to the Union League? I suspicion that between mining, sheriffing, Union League meetings, and now I reckon lodge meetings, you'll be away more than ever, where I can't take care of you."

"As I've told you, dear, my responsibilities to the territory are great. A man in my position is expected to join important organizations and to appear at social occasions to be seen and get to know influential people. It could mean a lot to us in the future."

"I don't care about any of that. I care about my husband being home at night where he belongs."

"Electa, it doesn't fall to you to tell me where I belong. I would think that you would be more sympathetic about the Southern support I've lost since joining the league and not so intent on criticizing me for supporting the community."

"Henry, I cannot continue like this," she said, facing him with her arms crossed. "I would like to return to the States at the earliest opportunity."

He stood up and said, "What? Are you certain-sure? We've been married but a month."

"I've given it a great deal of thought. I haven't made this decision lightly."

"I'm sure you haven't," he said quietly. "I will follow you after I sell the mines, but I can't say when that will be. I can't persuade you to stay?"

She shook her head. He took his hat from deer antlers he had nailed to the wall by the door and left. Alone again, Electa dried her hands and sat down at the table. She placed her head on her arms and sobbed, "Oh, how I miss Martha!" It seemed to her that such a drastic step would be necessary to force him away from a life that she feared would slowly kill him. If she stayed he would be gone more and more until they might as well not even be married. She felt a great loss, as though grieving the loss of her marriage that had hardly begun. Couldn't he understand that she needed him? Marriage was supposed to be for evenings at home and spending time with each other, not gallivanting all over town to meetings, or worse, over the country searching for lost cows.

Henry rode to his office in the back of Chrisman's store. It seemed to him that Electa was too demanding. He felt that she should understand that a man had certain obligations to the community, besides making a living. In his case, as he saw it, the two were one and the same. After all, he thought, a wife should support her husband, not complain about where and how he spends his time. He would talk to her again and convince her that she must stay. She would just have to put up with the situation. She would see that he was right in time. After all, the mines could hardly be doing better, and as soon as he could find enough carpenters, he would tell her of the new house he planned to build for her. Then he would petition Reverend Reed to send a preacher and gather support for the church she wanted so badly. He wondered if she wouldn't want a church even before her own comfort, and decided that yes, she surely would.

Chapter Twenty Two ~ Back at the Farm

"Martha, the cannon is ready," James said as he entered the house. "Why don't you and the children come outside for the celebration?"

"I don't believe I will," Martha said. She stood by the stove, poking boiling venison with a fork.

"But it's the Fourth of July," he said. "Come join us." He picked Harvey up, hoping that she would change her mind. He was worried about her. She hadn't been herself since Electa left.

"No, thank you, I don't feel much like celebrating," she sighed. "But the children want to watch, so please be careful, and make sure that they cover their ears. Have everyone come in after a while and I'll have supper on the table, such as it is," she sighed.

James thought she sighed too much, which couldn't be good, but he didn't blame her. Between their lack of supplies and Electa's leaving, everyone's spirits had fallen. It wasn't anyone's fault, really. He took Mary and Harvey outside, where Joseph and Francis waited at the cannon. Martha waited a minute or so and then looked out the door to make sure everyone was behind the cannon, just to make sure. She returned to her work and flinched when the cannon's report boomed.

"Too bad we don't have any fireworks," Joseph said. "Maybe next year." He wasn't much beyond being more than a boy himself, notwithstanding his size and missed the fanfare of parades, waving flags, and fireworks. The short celebration over, he and Francis lifted the cannon's tongue and pulled it to the barn.

That afternoon a small band of Blackfeet Indians appeared and wanted to camp inside the compound, but James wouldn't let them. He insisted that they remain outside which seemed to disturb them. They wanted food, but the Vails had shared all they could. Since James had given Henry the four paint ponies, they only had a few horses left. He wondered whether their uninvited guests might not try to take them or a few head of oxen. As a safeguard, he and Joseph took turns standing watch that night. In the morning, the rising sun found the band moving in the direction of St. Peter's Mission.

"Father Minatre should be all right with them. They won't hurt a priest," Joseph said as he went into the house for breakfast.

Joining him, James said, "If they had let me teach them how to grow corn and wheat, we would have had something to give them by now."

Two days later James ferried a family across the river that was on their way to Fort Benton for supplies. They brought news of an attack in Little Prickly Pear Canyon, presumably by Indians.

"There weren't no dead to bury," the man said. "Stuff was scattered all over, but we don't know what happened to nobody."

James asked them to stay in the compound for safety, but they refused and went on. He decided to go to Fort Benton himself, where, God willing, he would find their much-needed supplies or perhaps at least news of when the steamship would arrive. If not, he would be forced to do something else, but just what that might be he didn't know.

"I'm leaving for Fort Benton after dark," James announced at supper. "Francis, I'd be much obliged if you'd stay here with Joseph."

"Of course," Francis said.

Traveling at night for safety, he arrived at the fort two days later. He found the general store to be almost bare. He also found a man who claimed that several days earlier he'd been on a steamship but because of low water they couldn't continue on upstream. The captain had refused to take his cargo back to St. Louis, and decided to simply leave everything unloaded on the riverbank. He'd given his passengers a choice to either stay on the ship or to get off with the cargo. Many took whatever they could, disembarked, and walked, camping one hundred and fifty miles through dangerous country to Fort Benton.

"Was there a Reverend Reed on the ship?" asked James.

"There was, but I don't know that he got off. The captain said no more ships would be coming, so I wouldn't wait for him if I was you."

James wasn't going to wait because it was impossible to know whether the man that had hired them would arrive with their pay or not. But before leaving he searched the fort and then rode the riverbank looking for the good Reverend. For the entire trip back he regretted that upon his homecoming, he'd have to relate his sad report. Joseph, working by the barn, saw him open the gate.

"Hello, James," he called.

James waved a greeting and noticed a strange contraption by the barn. He walked his horse to the house where Joseph met him.

"Joseph, it's good to be back, but I'm sorry to say that there was no ship, no supplies, no Reverend Reed, and I still can't pay you your wages."

"Well, I never expected this," Joseph said, scratching his head. "I don't know what to say or do."

"I've had some time to think about it," James said. "I can't expect you to stay on. I don't even know when I could pay you cash money. But I would appreciate it if you'd take the six oxen for pay. I'd feel that at least I'd been fair."

"Thank you. I believe I'll take that offer."

"Good. What is that thing over there?" James said, pointing at the contraption. Joseph grinned. "Why don't you go in and see your family? Francis will want to show it off himself," he teased. James went into the house where he found Francis eating supper.

"Did you see my outfit?" Francis asked.

"Is that what it is?" Martha said with a rare tease. She gave James a welcome home kiss before he hugged Mary and Harvey.

As he ate, he shared what had happened and the fact that Joseph was leaving, which further upset Martha. She lived close to tears every day already. James gave her a comforting hug before the men went out to see Francis's outfit. He had tied two pine poles wide enough apart to fit on the sides of a horse to the opposite sides of a sturdy wood dry-goods box. Bolted to each side of the box were two round iron pulleys for wheels. On the horse end, wide strips of buffalo hide hung loosely across the poles to serve as a kind of harness.

"I've not seen anything like it. What's it for?" James said.

"It's time for me to leave as well, James. I must find a place to do business and then recover my goods that were on that steamship. I don't like riding a horse, and I don't have a wagon, so I made this."

"It looks like a real go-devil," James said, chuckling. "When will you leave?"

"First light tomorrow. I'll head for Cottonwood on the way to Bannock. Perhaps I can find a place there that would do for a store; if not, I'll build one. After I find a place to do business I'll come back through here with a few supplies."

"That's kind of you," James said. "You know how hard it's been on everyone, and we'd be much obliged. You know, we may be forced to leave the farm." Francis merely nodded.

The next morning, the remaining Vail family watched Francis, who stood in his go-devil being pulled by a mare, ride proudly, though slowly, through the compound and out the gate. Joseph had decided to follow on horseback and push his oxen along. James walked behind the odd ensemble as far as the gate and waved before closing it behind them. The little band followed the Missouri River south for three days before heading southwest. Pushing oxen was slow going. It took an entire week to reach Cottonwood, where Joseph sold all six oxen at such a tidy sum that Francis asked him to be his partner in trade. He agreed.

Several more days on the trail brought them to Bannock. Finding two empty buildings on Main Street that had been vacated by two brothers named Stuart, they claimed them for the business; bought a wagon, team, and supplies; and directly found the Plummer residence. Francis knocked on the door, which Electa opened.

"Francis! Joseph!" she happily exclaimed. "Please come in! It's so good to see you. What are you doing in Bannock?"

The two men removed their hats, and upon entering, Francis noticed how clean and organized the small cabin was. Joseph felt uncomfortable. He sat on the table bench and looked around the unfamiliar place, trying to imagine Henry at home there. Electa made fresh coffee while they told her all that had happened. Her eyes became misty with tears, and she dabbed at them with her apron. Concerned, the men exchanged a glance.

"Is life as Mrs. Henry Plummer that terrible?" Francis teased, not knowing whether it was the right thing to say or not.

"It's not Bannock, such as it is," she said, implying that the place was less than she would have liked. "But I will admit that married life with Henry isn't what I had hoped it would be. First I missed my home in Ohio. By God's grace I conquered that, and now I miss Martha just as terribly. But I know that God helped me before, and He will again," she sighed.

"I'm sure of that," Francis said, trying to encourage her.

"Francis, I'm as lonely as ever. I try not to show my sadness when Henry is home, but that's not very often, I'm afraid. It seems as if every miner within one hundred miles needs his attention. Besides tending to his own mines there are Union League meetings, saloon shootings, and there is no jail. What is Henry to do? What am I to do?"

"I'm sure Henry's up to it, ma'am," Joseph said.

"Of that I'm certain," Electa said, "but I don't know that I am. I expected him to come home at night, not ramble all over the territory. He apparently thinks more of others than he does of his own wife."

Embarrassed, the men looked at each other again. It occurred to Joseph that the room had suddenly become quite warm, and he turned slightly red. Francis rubbed his hands together slowly, pursed his lips, and thought about her situation.

"Well," he said, "I recall Henry's concern for his responsibilities when at the farm. It seems that your husband is a very hard-working, conscientious young man."

"In Ohio that would have been wonderful. At least he would have been home every night. But here, I never know if or when to expect him. He'd tell me if he knew, but when he goes out only God knows when I'll see him again."

"Please take this as well as I mean it, Electa," Francis said, and paused to let her prepare herself for what he was about to say. She looked at him apprehensively. "You have more faith in God than anyone I know. Don't let it fail you now."

"Thank you, Francis. I'll think about what you've said."

"We're leaving immediately for the Missouri," Francis said. "We'll stop at the farm with supplies, and tell the family we saw you."

"Please tell them I miss them, but that I'm fine," she cautioned.

"Of course," he said.

They left for Sun River Farm, where they arrived in less than a week. They found the Vails safe and grateful for the food and news they brought.

"Thank you both for bringing news of Electa," Martha said, smiling as she set the table. "You've lifted my spirits. I'm so relieved to hear that she's doing well. It sounds like Henry is real busy. It's been so long since we've had anything to eat besides meat and corn meal that I almost forgot how to cook."

"That will be the day, when you forget how to cook," Joseph said.

"That's right Martha," Francis agreed. "The least we could do for you after cooking all those meals for us was to bring you a few supplies," he teased.

"But the prices!" Martha said. "Flour for ten dollars a hundred pound! Land sakes. And sugar at eighty cents per pound and coffee at ninety! I'm afraid that we'll be forever repaying you."

"Nonsense," Francis said. "Friends don't repay friends but with friendship."

"What are your plans?" James asked.

"If Joseph doesn't mind, I'm going to stay over for a few day's rest while he goes on to the Missouri to retrieve the goods I ordered. I'll follow along to get whatever he can't carry, while he comes back through here on his way to Bannock. We want to start business by summer's end."

After supper the men went to the barn to tend the horses.

"Have you decided what you'll do, James?" Francis asked.

"We can stay here and have another starvation winter. Or we can go to Fort Benton, where it's so crowded that we'd be worse off than staying here. Perhaps we should join you and the Plummers at Bannock. I could find work, and Martha would have plenty of supplies to cook with," he grinned. "Besides, she and Electa would be happy to be able to see each other again."

"That's true," Francis said. "It's obvious that they miss each other terribly. The only wise choice is Bannock. Why not come with me? There is safety in numbers. We'll go through Cottonwood. It's about halfway and a good place to rest."

"I'll tell Martha," James said.

Francis and Joseph followed their plan. Joseph went ahead to the Missouri River, found the drop-off place, packed the wagon with boxes of goods, and headed back, but somehow missed Francis on the trail. It took Joseph over a week to return to Sun River Farm, and only stopped for one night before going on to Bannock. It was the first week of August before Francis appeared at the farm with yet more goods packed on his horse riding his go-devil. James had packed a wagon with all their worldly goods. Martha usually followed James without question, but she insisted that they follow Henry and Electa's route to Bannock so she could "see what she saw and feel what she felt." James assented against his better judgment. The next morning, Francis and the Vails left the farm. James ferried Francis across the Sun River.

"I wonder which of us will reach Bannock City first?" James said, teasing.

"It doesn't matter, so long as we all arrive safe and sound," Francis said. "So let us both watch for Indians."

"Agreed," James said, and they shook hands before he returned back across the river for Martha and the children.

Chapter Twenty-Three ~ Glorious Reunion

Henry had been severely disappointed when he discovered an archenemy in Nathaniel P. Langford, the thirty-one year old president of the Union League. A United States Marshal by the name of Payne had ridden into Bannock with the idea in his mind of having a representative from the east side of the territory in the Idaho legislature. Since Langford held the Union League's highest position, Payne felt that he was the best candidate, and planned to nominate him for representative. At the same time, Payne conceived of the appointment of a Deputy United States Marshal to be headquartered in Bannock. He left it up to the thirty-odd Union League members to choose the man. Their choice by secret ballot: Sheriff Henry Plummer. Langford had never been particularly friendly to Henry, and made his animosity apparent by refusing to approve the vote. Payne left Bannock as sorely disappointed as both Langford and Henry, who resigned his Union League membership and never again spoke to Langford.

Fearful of Indian attack, James wasted no time following the Plummer's route. He refused to stay at the Dearborn River the first night as the newlyweds had, pausing at the campsite only long enough to eat supper.

"But James," Martha protested, "such long days in the wagon will tire us excessively. It's so nice here by the river. Can't we stop and rest for the night?"

"Dear, I know you want to camp where Electa did, but please understand that safety must come first. We're not in the compound now. And I'm going to do everything I can to lessen the chance that we'll happen across an unfriendly band of Blackfeet."

Martha sighed. "You're right, of course, dear. I didn't mean to be foolish. We have the children to think of, as well as Electa and ourselves."

James kept his family traveling at a stubborn pace, arriving in Bannock in only five days. They descended off the hill and entered Main Street about midafternoon. They passed men lounging in front of saloons and exchanged waves and nods with them.

"One would think a woman might be seen on Main Street," Martha said. "I wonder where Electa and Henry are staying?"

"The place isn't as hectic as I thought it would be," James said. "Some of these buildings are empty. I wonder what has happened. We need to find out where the Plummers place is and then find one of our own."

"I imagine they would have us for one night, at least," Martha said.

"We'll see," he replied. He reined up the horses in front of the Goodrich Hotel. Another of Henry's deputies, Buck Stinson, had just crossed the street, and reached the door just as James stepped down.

"Excuse me, sir," James said. "Can you tell me where the Plummers live?"

"He's my boss, so I reckon I should be able to," Stinson said, touching his hat brim and nodding to Martha. "Turn right at the next street. Cross the ditch. It's the third place on the right."

"Much obliged," James said, as the deputy tipped his hat to Martha and went inside. A few minutes later, Electa opened the door when she heard the horses outside.

"Martha!" she cried, and ran to the wagon. "Oh, Martha! I'm so glad you're here. Hello, dears," she said kindly to the children, caressing Mary's hair. "Come here, Harvey, so Mother can get down. Henry isn't here right now, but he may be back tonight. I honestly never know when to expect him. Hello, James."

"Hello, sister, it's good to see you again," he said, and helped Martha down.

The women happily hugged and cried before going inside.

"Ladies, if you'll excuse me, I'm going to find us a house," James said.

"Not yet, you won't," Electa insisted. "You'll come in first and have a cup of fresh, hot coffee. I'm not going to have it said that you went poking around town before even coming into my house."

"All right, but then I'll have to go. Henry might come home and be alarmed at finding a tribe camped in his parlor."

"No more surprised than I would be to see him home for a change. He's home twice a week, maybe. Besides," Electa teased, "as many years as I lived with you, and as many meals as Henry took with us, I think we could stand to have the Vails in our home for one night."

An hour later, James had found a large suitable cabin across Grasshopper Creek on Yankee Flat. The women had supper prepared by the time he returned, and that evening, Electa helped them get settled in their new home. Unloading the wagon, James carried a box inside, and sat down on a crate in the parlor, where Electa folded linen.

"I can't bear to cook alone any longer," she said. "It's silly for us to have separate meals at both places. Martha and I simply must prepare our meals together just as we always have. Henry will have to allow it. I'm sure he'll understand." The sisters had every intention of spending as much time together as possible.

"That's fine," James said, "but just how will we menfolk know where to find our next meal; here or at your place?" he teased.

"Well," Martha said from the kitchen, "we do have more room. I think it will be a nice change of pace for Electa to come here."

"I agree," Electa said, grinning, but her impish grin quickly melted, as she became somber. "Then it's settled," she said. "We'll cook and have meals together for as long as I'm here." She hadn't really planned on saying anything, but suddenly the time seemed right. Now that she had been reunited with family she didn't want any unnecessary secrets between them. They had to be told of her leaving eventually, and she thought the sooner the better.

"What do you mean," Martha said, "for as long as you're here?" She set her dishes down and went to the doorway separating the two rooms. At her appearance, Electa stopped what she was doing, looked at them both and then at the linen.

"I think it best that you know right away," she said. "I have told Henry that I would like to go back to the States, and he has consented."

"Go back to the States?" Martha said. "But why would you do such a thing?"

"Henry is gone so much that I cannot continue living here."

"Why?" Martha said. "Even with us here? My dear, you can move in with us for companionship. We'd love to have you with us again, wouldn't we James?"

"Of course. In fact, we refuse to take no for an answer," he said.

"Thank you. I do appreciate your carefulness," Electa said, "but that wouldn't solve anything. We would all be in the same circumstances as at the farm, except that Henry and I are husband and wife. Don't you see? Marriage means little to me unless my husband comes home at night. Henry comes and goes as though our home is a roadside inn. He's gone so much that I have imposed myself upon your family before you've even unpacked."

"You could never impose upon us, dear," Martha said gently.

"You know how we feel about you," James said. "Unfortunately for your situation, we'll be returning to Sun River as soon as I can get supplies, but have no idea when that will be. You'd be as welcome as the flowers in springtime." She gave him a small smile at that.

"Of course I know that," she said.

"Henry will settle down in time," Martha said.

"No," Electa said, shaking her head. "His sense of duty is clear as he sees it. Both his duties and interests increase regularly. Nothing will prevent him, not even his wife, so I see no purpose in continuing our present situation."

"Oh, my dear," Martha said, "please don't go. Surely the Lord wouldn't want you to. Everything within me cautions you not to leave."

"I'm afraid I must."

"Electa, are you certain-sure about this?" James asked.

"I've thought it all quite through," she said quietly. "As dutiful as Henry is, I believe he will join me after he takes care of his business interests. I believe that with all my heart."

Martha said imploringly, "Please, dear, I admonish you not to do this." She sighed. "But if you must go away, I'm sure he will join you when he can," Martha said, surrendering her own will to Electa's, and she moved to comfort her with a hug.

"Do you know yet when you'll leave?" James said, as he turned to go.

"No," Electa said. "The next time the stage arrives from Salt Lake."

James went outside as the women hugged again. Tears welled up in their eyes and together they began to sob heavily.

~

Henry returned to Bannock several days later. He gladly assented to taking meals with Electa at the Vails, as he knew it made her happy. Henry had just left Chrisman's store where he had an office of sorts, when he saw Francis approaching slowly on horseback.

"Greetings, Henry," Francis said. "How is Electa keeping you these days?"

"Fine as frog's hair, Francis. Come in from Cottonwood?"

"I did. You'd be proud of me, too, I dare say. Led a group of men into town."

"Who might that be?" Henry asked, always interested in new arrivals.

"They said they know you from west of here. Red Yeager, Marshland, Zachary, and Doc Howard, to name a few." Henry frowned and shook his head in disgust.

"Thompson, those men are cutthroats and robbers. Hell will be to pay now!"

"What could you possibly mean, Plummer? They were more than pleasant on the way here, and did me good service. They also spoke very well of you, I might add."

"They speak well of me for they don't dare do otherwise," Henry replied.

"Oh, that's right, your reputation," Francis said, nodding.

"What of it?" Henry said. "Few things said of a man are entirely true. Electa knows the truth and married me anyway, or because of it. And neither one of us knows a more honest creature."

"True enough," Francis said. "You've proven to me that you're as good as many men, and better than most I've known."

"Thank you, Francis," Henry said, looking around. "But I still regret your bringing those men here. I'll have to watch my back now. Where did you leave them?"

"I believe they entered the Elkhorn Saloon," Francis said.

"Much obliged. By the way, the Vails arrived a few days ago. They're over on Yankee Flat, the first big house."

"Much obliged, yourself. I'll find them tomorrow, after I get settled. I hope my friends don't cause you too much trouble. Be seeing you," Francis said, and reined his horse while kicking his flanks.

Henry touched his hat brim, grinned, and continued his measured, careful stroll up the street. Francis had turned his horse the other way toward the hotel. The next morning after breakfast, he went for a walk to find the Vails on Yankee Flat.

Before reaching the narrow footbridge at the end of town, he saw Electa and crossed the street to talk to her.

"Electa! How wonderful to see you!" he said, taking his hat off.

"Francis, thank you! When did you get here?" she said.

"Yesterday. Didn't Henry mention that we had talked when I arrived?"

"No, he didn't. He's not in town that often, so we have many things to discuss when he's home," she said. "It probably slipped his mind. By the way, I'm leaving Bannock myself."

"Leaving?" he exclaimed. "But why?"

"Regretfully, Henry is away from home so much attending to his duties as sheriff, that I have asked to go home to family in Iowa." Francis looked startled. "He has consented," she assured him, "and will join me after taking care of his business."

"Well, I must say that I am surprised," he said.

"No more than I," she said. "I had hoped for much from Bannock, but the place is so wild," she said, shaking her head. "I can tolerate no churches or schools, but I won't stand for no husband." He nodded his understanding and remembered their earlier conversation. "Have you seen the Vails yet?" she said, changing the subject.

"No, not yet. I understand their place is across the bridge," he said.

"Yes, the first big house. Martha will be glad to see you, Francis. I know she's home; let's go together so we can talk some more."

"All right, let's go see Martha," he said, smiling, and she laughed.

James was gone, but Martha opened the door.

"Francis! Electa! Land sakes, come in!" she said. They could tell from her eyes that she had been crying.

"Hello, Martha, it's good to see you," he said, taking off his hat. He moved aside and allowed Electa to go in first. She stepped into Martha's arms. They cried softly together while Francis turned his hat around in his hands and looked at the hills.

"Forgive me, Francis," Martha said, stepping back and looking at Electa, "but Electa is in quite a fix, and we women must have our moments while there's time."

"Of course," he said.

They followed her to the kitchen where they sat down at the table while she poured them a cup of hot coffee.

"Have you found a place to stay, Francis?"

"No, not yet; I just got into town yesterday," he said, sipping his coffee.

"Well," Martha said, "with half the town gone to the new camp, we found this nice big house empty, and had just fairly decided to take in boarders. It would be a blessing if you would be one. We know each other and it would be nice to have you eat with us, just like at the farm. Besides, I have plenty of supplies now."

He chuckled and said, "I hope you won't fix corn bread for awhile."

"Francis!" she said, blushing. "You know I'm embarrassed about all that corn bread!"

"I'd be proud to take meals here, if I can afford it. How much would you need to have?"

"For you, and Joseph too, if he's with you," she paused, waiting for an answer.

"He will be," Francis chuckled. He and Electa exchanged a grin.

"Then how about ten dollars each per week? Is that fair enough?" Martha said.

"That would be fine. Thank you for the invitation and the coffee. Say, is supper the same time as always?" he said, and they all laughed.

They heard the front door open, some footsteps, and it shut again.

"Look what the cat dragged in," James said from the parlor. Henry appeared in the doorway looking more grim than pleased.

"Hello, dear. What's wrong?" Electa said.

"The Salt Lake City stage just got into town," he said.

Chapter Twenty Four ~ Parting Sentiments

Henry's unavoidable words seemed to echo in Electa's mind as he stopped just inside the kitchen. James followed him as far as the doorway and leaned against it. An uncomfortable silence filled the kitchen.

"When will it be leaving?" Electa finally said solemnly.

"Tomorrow morning. One more evening together," Henry replied, not taking his eyes off her. She met his gaze, which made her eyes glisten with tears.

"Are you all right, dear?" Martha said. Electa nodded as she wiped her eyes with a white handkerchief. "Would you like coffee, Henry? James?"

"No, thank you," James said. "I'll wait in the parlor until supper." He left the room while Henry nodded, not as a yes, but in agreement with James. He broke his gaze at Electa and followed James to the parlor where they sat down on the couch. They spoke in quiet tones.

"Any chance Electa will postpone her trip?" James said.

Henry slowly shook his head. "No. She asked me how many more stages there would be this year. I had to tell her that there is no way of knowing. That this could be the last one, but I doubt it."

"Do you think she'll be on it?" James said. Henry nodded in the affirmative.

"Yes," he said thoughtfully. "Yes, I do."

"Well, my friend," James said, "I don't envy you. Not that it matters, but rumors are all over town about her leaving. I've heard all kinds of stories and guesses. You know how it is."

"Yes, I know. And knowing my own faults as I do and dealing with the baser element of society, there are times when I truly tire of our race. But I am obliged that I married a fine example of the better element."

The men watched the women prepar supper; they busily moved from the stove to the table to the cupboards and then back again, stirring, pouring, and setting, as they had done together so many times before. Joseph arrived before very long, knocked, took off his hat, and entered. He shook hands with the two men on his way through the parlor to the kitchen, where he settled in for coffee with Francis.

"Is it true, Electa? That you're leaving, I mean?" Joseph said.

"Yes, it is. Henry's many responsibilities have given me the chance to return to family. Until he can join me, of course," she added. Martha went to the parlor door.

"James, Henry, supper is ready. Please come in," she said.

"Well, ma'am," Joseph said, "I'll sure be sorry to see you go." Electa gave him a weak smile.

"Thank you, you're a sweet dear," she said, which embarrassed him, but he didn't mind. James took his place at one end of the long table and Henry sat down on a bench next to Electa.

"Let us thank God for the food and pray for Electa's journey," James said. "Mary and Harvey, bow your heads. Shall we join hands?" Electa wouldn't look at Henry as he took her hand.

"Heavenly Father," James prayed, "thank You for friends around a table of Your supply. Bless the hands that prepared the food to the nourishment of our bodies. Grant our dear Electa journey mercies as she leaves us. Please give her safety over the many miles of trail she is about to cross. Amen."

It was a rather calm supper, compared to the happy chatter and spirited conversation they had so often enjoyed together. Even the children behaved themselves, perhaps subdued by the somber mood. Afterwards, Electa insisted on cleaning up with Martha before going home. "That was our agreement," she said. She and Martha remained composed while they quietly talked and the men drank coffee, but tears again surfaced when Henry and Electa prepared to leave. Joseph and Francis chose to remain in the kitchen and drink coffee to give the women privacy while they hugged at the door.

"Shall we see you in the morning?" Martha said.

"Of course, dear," Electa replied. "We'll come over for breakfast. By then I might know what time the stage is leaving." She hugged James and the children, said goodnight, and they left. Neither Henry nor Electa said a word until they reached Grasshopper Creek and the footbridge.

"Henry, will you try to find out tonight what time I need to be ready?" Electa said.

He nodded and said; "I'll find the driver after I take you home, even if I have to wake him."

She smiled at that. If he were only that considerate when it came to his job, she would stay. But, she reckoned that a man's true character shines at his work. She wouldn't want a slothful husband, and thanked God that she could be proud of Henry for that. But she couldn't have what she wanted and what she felt that she had to have, so she would leave. He got her safely home and left to find the stage driver. She got into bed before he returned, but his errand didn't take long. She had left a single lamp burning for him, which threw large shadows around the room. He stopped inside the door and wondered whether she was still awake.

"Thank you, Henry," she said, answering his uncertainty.

"I found him. I reckon he's still sober enough to remember that he has a job in the morning," he said quietly. He didn't want to disturb her. She had a rough trip ahead. Francis had made it before and had warned her of the hardships she faced.

"I will miss you," she said. He paused, concentrating on her small voice, embedding it in his mind so he would remember it.

"And I you," he replied, still standing by the door.

"Will you ever forgive me?" she said.

"Forgive what?" he said.

"I will be forever convinced that God has brought us together," she said. "And I, without His permission, am separating us. Will you ever forgive my stubborn selfishness?"

"The frontier life hasn't been easy for you," he said. "Poor food, Indians, infernal isolation. Neither one of us can help the way we feel. You can't help your desires and I can't deny what I am. Whatever happens, I will count our short time together as the finest of my life. There's nothing to forgive. I have something for you," he said, and moved to the bed, where he sat down and placed several small leather bags between them on the blanket. "Pokes of gold dust," he explained. "Hide it on your person in case your trunk is lost. Or, God help him, some fool tries to rob you," he teased, and began to take his boots off.

She sat up in the small bed, revealing her bare shoulders. At her movement, he turned and saw yellow locks of hair curled around a few of her fingers, which shone as gold in the dim lamplight. She fixed her eyes on his for a long moment.

"I shall cherish our last night of privacy together," she said, "for we shall have none on the trail."

~

In the morning, Henry carried Electa's trunk to the Goodrich on their way to the Vails. Everyone knew that breakfast would be more of the same sorrow and tears that supper had been. After another subdued meal, hands were shaken, hugs given again, and last good-byes said at the door. Electa held a red lap blanket Martha had given her for the journey. Distraught, Martha couldn't bear to see her ride away on yet another wagon. She fairly fainted from grief, so James helped her to their room. He kissed her on a teary-wet cheek and left her alone, lying on the bed sobbing.

"She'll be all right," James said when he came out. Henry nodded his understanding while Electa silently dabbed her eyes with a handkerchief and clung to her keepsake blanket.

"Would you like me or Joseph to stay while you see Electa off?" Francis said.

"No, thank you," James replied. "She didn't sleep last night. I imagine she will now. We should leave. It's almost time."

They filed outside where Joseph, odd man out, walked alone at the rear behind James and Francis and the parting couple. A cool morning, smoke rose from chimneys all over town. Single file again, they crossed the narrow double-log footbridge and walked the block to the Goodrich, where the stage waited. Called a stage, the open, two-mule, triple-seated wagon had other passengers waiting, a man and a woman.

"There won't be smooth sailing on that farm cart," Francis said as they approached. "That wagon hasn't any springs." Henry frowned and shook his head in disgust.

"It's not even a one-horse outfit," he said. "Two mules and stiff seats."

"I can use my new blanket as a cushion, so it's no trouble," Electa said matter-of-factly. "It will still get us there, won't it?" Henry looked at James, whose eyebrows raised at the question.

"That remains to be seen," James said. "I don't like your chances. What's the driver like, Henry? Is he capable of defending his passengers against hostiles and bandits?"

"I don't like the odds either," Henry said. "To make sure, I'm going to tag along for a few days." James glanced at Electa, who didn't appear to be surprised, so he reckoned she already knew of Henry's intent.

He looked across and down the street toward Chrisman's store; saw Henry's horse saddled, and ready to travel. Deputy Buck Stinson came outside, took the reins, and began leading the horse toward them. Henry reckoned that the other passengers would buffer the breeze somewhat, so he helped Electa up into the rear seat. James caught Joseph's eye and motioned at Electa's trunk. Together, they lifted it up behind Electa's seat. The other passengers got settled in the wagon, and Buck arrived with Henry's horse.

"Much obliged, Buck," Henry said.

The deputy simply nodded and said "Ma'am," while lifting his hat in respect.

James stepped up to the wagon where she sat. She leaned over and he kissed her cheek. "Goodbye, dear. Godspeed," he said.

"Tell Martha I'll be fine," she said, to which he nodded his compliance.

Joseph took off his hat, stepped up, and smiling, silently shook her hand. Francis took his turn and said, "Remember that you'll always be welcome in the West. You'll be missed, Electa." She wiped a tear away and took a deep breath before quietly thanking him.

"See you when you get back, Henry," Buck said. "Keep your powder dry."

"You do the same," Henry said. "You boys trade off Bannock duty while I'm gone. Whoever isn't here is to be in Alder Gulch. You can stay at Rattlesnake Ranch one night at a time if you want. But that Red Yeager has hired on and I reckon he's trouble."

"You bet, Henry. We'll hold the fort," Buck said.

"See that you do," Henry said, mounting his horse. "The last time I left the country, Dillingham got killed. Someone will pay the devil if I lose another deputy."

Buck nodded and stepped back to let Henry's horse by. The stage driver showed up and climbed into the front seat, where he picked up the reins and glanced around. He spat black tobacco juice on the ground and looked Henry up and down.

"You goin' along, mister?" he said.

All eyes turned to Henry, who just nodded. The driver slapped the reins on the pitiful mule's backs. "Sarah! Missy!" he yelled. "Giddyap there!"

Chapter Twenty Five ~ The Last Good-bye

Electa gave James, Francis, and Joseph one last small smile, which they all returned and waved good-bye.

"Be seeing you, Henry," James said, at which Henry, expressionless, simply nodded.   He nudged his horse and followed behind the wagon as it headed south out of town across Grasshopper Creek, bound for Salt Lake City.

Henry rode in disbelieving disgust that a man with any sense would use gaunt animals in such an enterprise. Stage customers expected to get where they were going, but Henry angrily wondered whether the scrawny animals would make it.   The small party topped the first hill and a wide expanse of sagebrush opened up before them. Mountains rimmed the horizon in every direction. An annoying, fine dust rose slowly around and behind the wagon, which practically blinded the passengers and made them cough. Henry dampened a handkerchief at his canteen's mouth and leaned away from his horse to hand it to Electa. She gratefully took it and placed it over her nose and mouth. "Francis had been right," she thought; "it would be a hard trip."

Henry, the same handsome, romantic figure she had been pleasured to see before on picnics and their journey to the falls, rode at her side, but away from the dust-stirring wagon.   A connoisseur of horseflesh, he insisted on the finest mount he could afford. The ears of his spirited bay pointed ever forward as the athletic animal pranced through the sagebrush, holding his tail high. Henry continually watched for any form of danger, but he studied his wife more than she knew. He looked for some weakness in her resolve, but found none. She remained steadfast in her dogged determination, even among such arduous circumstances.

The dusty miles relented stubbornly and slowly. Martha had packed enough food for them both in a cloth bag of sorts, but dust infiltrated everything; the bag, the food, the passengers' eyes, ears, noses, clothing, even the clothes they had packed in presumably secure trunks. The dust spared only Henry as he rode apart from the wagon.

Electa felt relieved and thankful for that, since she already feared for his well-being. His mulish insistence upon working unreasonable hours for days on end coupled with the onset of cool weather had caused his consumptive cough to worsen. He also had begun to lose weight. In Bannock she had considered protesting his escort, but knew her words would have been in vain. But not even Henry could deny that sleeping outside injured his health.

The land evened out somewhat on the third day. In the afternoon, magnificent mountain peaks of solid gray rock could be seen rising into the eastern sky. Henry noticed Electa admiring them.

"They're the Teton Peaks. Nothing like them in the States," he said to which she offered no reply.

After almost a week of the insufferable dust, the party passed Market Lake and reached the Snake River. There water swirled under ropes that had been stretched across the river. Rafts carried single wagons at a time.

"Henry, what is this place called?" Electa said.

"Eagle Rock," he replied. "They come here to catch fish."

The crossing reminded Electa of the Sun River Farm. A small wagon train six strong had crossed, and their wagon master had waited behind to help two more independent wagons. Each one appeared to hold a family. The wagon master already had one across sitting on the riverbank, driven by a handsome young man with brown hair, beard, and mustache. As Electa's stage approached, the second wagon pulled in to the landing.

"Hello, the north shore!" a white-bearded older gentleman called from the raft. He wore black pants and a vest over a well-worn shirt.

"Hello yourself!" Electa's stage driver replied as he reined the mules up. The young driver of the waiting wagon nodded to

Henry, and in just a few minutes, the elder stranger's wagon had disembarked the raft. The women appeared to be visibly relieved to be on solid ground again. The younger man got down to shake Henry's hand, apparently in lieu of the entire party. He introduced his family first and then himself, and said he was Wilbur Fisk Sanders. Henry introduced himself and Electa and the other two passengers followed suit.

"I'm pleased to meet an officer of the law," Sanders said. "Allow me to introduce my uncle and his family, Chief Justice of Idaho Territory and Mrs. Sidney Edgerton; and their two boys, Wright and Sidney. Mr. Edgerton's ward Henry Tilden is fifteen, old enough to help us drive the wagons," he said teasing. "The Edgerton's daughter Pauline is five; Martha, a young lady in her own right is thirteen; and the slightly older young lady is the Chief Justice's niece, Miss Lucia Darling."

Henry wasn't lost on Sanders's meaning that the old man outranked a sheriff. But it didn't bother him. He didn't reckon it would affect him one way or the other. He answered to the miner's court and expected to continue doing so. But Henry did wonder why the man had come. He took off his hat in respect before speaking.

"Pleased to make your acquaintance," Henry said. "Mr. Edgerton, sir, may I ask what your destination is?"

"You may," the politician said. "Even in this wilderness, you know by now that our government formed Idaho Territory this spring, partly from eastern Washington Territory, and partly from western Dakota Territory."

Henry nodded his understanding and patiently waited for the man's point.

"The difficulty," he continued, "is that there are now two towns that claim the name of Bannock in the new Idaho Territory," he said smiling. "Right now they are called East Bannock and West Bannock, which is unsatisfactory. One or the other must change its name," he said, implying that he would be instrumental in the decision.

"I see," Henry said, while noticing that the driver had loaded the stage onto the ferry.

"President Lincoln has appointed me Chief Justice of Idaho Territory, and I am especially interested in the development of the towns east of the divide. And you, sir, to what political party do you subscribe?"

"Sir, I am proud to say that I am a loyal Union Democrat," Henry said. "But I trust that, if you and your party settle east of the Divide, we can work together agreeably. I look forward to discussing matters with you, sir, but at the moment I have pressing private business, if you will kindly excuse me." He put his hat back on and touched the brim for the women. "Ladies," he said, and nudging his horse, rode the short distance to the ferry and dismounted.

He helped Electa down from her seat so they could go for one last walk together while the ferryman secured the stage on the raft. The wagon master, a seasoned mountain man who wore fringed buckskins and a round-brimmed black hat, approached Edgerton as the couple walked off alone.

"Who did that jasper say he is?" the wagon master said.

"Sheriff Henry Plummer of East Bannock," Edgerton said. "Why? Do you know him?"

"I know of him. I was in California a few years back when he was the sheriff there. He shot a man over a difficulty with a woman and was sent to prison. Don't know how he got out or what he's done since, but I reckoned you should know if you're going into his country."

"I see," Edgerton said. "Sir, I appreciate you informing me of the sheriff's past. He certainly seems to be a man who bears watching."

"Real close, I'd say," the wagon master replied. He gave Edgerton a wink and a nod, mounted his horse, and rode away after his wagon train. Nephew Sanders walked up to the Chief Justice.

"What did the wagon master want?" Sanders said.

"To warn us about our new friend, the good Sheriff Henry Plummer. It seems that he has been in prison for murder in California."

Surprised, Sanders said, "Can we dare trust such a man?"

"No, nephew, we dare not. If Mr. Plummer thinks he can pull the wool over the eyes of this Chief Justice, he is sadly mistaken. By the way, I wonder why his wife is leaving the territory?" They looked at the young couple walking together by the river.

~

"Electa, I don't know what else to say," Henry said. "You've been distant since we left Bannock. If I could have one wish, it would be that you would stay."

"To be honest with you, leaving is against my better judgment," Electa said. "I haven't written Victoria for some time for fear she would chastise me for doing so. She would say that I finally realized my dreams from God and now I'm leaving them for little reason. I don't expect her to understand. Henry, I'm leaving so that you'll follow me, and save your life. I can't bear for you to work yourself to death. I won't watch it. Perhaps absence will make our hearts grow fonder. Will you join me when you can?"

"I can't promise when," he said. "Selling the mines may be easier said than done. I don't understand your reckoning, but I do appreciate why you're doing it." He looked around, took a deep breath, and coughed several times. She stopped walking, and he turned to face her.

"You will promise me that you'll take care of yourself, won't you?" Electa said. "And that you'll eat with James and Martha and let her take care of you?" He smiled at her concern.

"Mrs. Plummer, you are a puzzle. A conundrum I doubt I shall ever solve," he teased. "I will miss you as I have never missed anyone. Will you pray for me?"

"Of course and always," she said. "You've never asked me that before."

"You know I'm not a fearful man, but I suspicion that I shall never see you again," he said, half teasing. "Of that I am indeed afraid."

"Don't be silly, of course you will. After you sell the mines and follow me," she said smiling. He gently took her hands in his own and kissed each one before looking into her eyes. They kissed for what seemed a long time to Sanders. He saw her wipe a tear away before the couple turned and began their return walk to the ferry.

"Sheriff Plummer, we're going to go on ahead," Edgerton called out. Henry waved his acknowledgment, and the men snapped their reins and the wagons began to move. When the couple reached the ferry, Henry helped Electa onto the raft and up into the wagon. She turned to him and their eyes met once again.

"Good bye my love," she whispered.

"Godspeed," he replied quietly, and kissed her hand for perhaps the last time. He gently squeezed it, let it go, stepped off the raft, and picked up the reins to his horse. The ferryman shoved off. Henry mounted his horse and sat there until they had crossed and unloaded the wagon. He waved a heavy hand before turning his horse's head and nudging him up the trail to Bannock.

Within an hour he had caught up to the Edgerton party without trying. He didn't feel much like talking, but thought it the polite thing to do with folks new to the country. Besides, he reckoned a man as powerful as Chief Justice of the Territory had come to do more than just change the name of a town. He wanted to ride close enough to talk to both men, but far enough away to stay out of the dust, so he stayed by Edgerton's wagon, which led Sanders's.

"Mr. Edgerton," Henry said, "I hear tell that President Lincoln himself has been fairly captured by the Confederate

Army," which made Edgerton laugh heartily. Sanders smiled, which Henry thought might be unusual.

"And why aren't you fighting for the Union, Sheriff?" Sanders said. Henry grinned.

"That bee's nest is the rich man's war and the poor man's fight," Henry said. "I was out here before anyone kicked the nest over and stirred things up. Besides, there are different ways to fight." At that, Henry noticed Edgerton turn around to look at Sanders.

"Just what do you mean by that?" Sanders asked.

Henry ignored the question and said, "Why come out here with your uncle instead of joining the fight yourself?" Sanders thought Henry's question rude, and paid no attention to it.

"Tell me, Sheriff," Edgerton said, "what is Bannock, that is, East Bannock, like?"

Henry smiled inside. "Mr. Edgerton, you probably have a surprise on the horizon. I reckon that she's not like any town you've been to."

"How so?" Sanders said, curious, which made Henry want to laugh, but didn't.

"She was born of greed, which isn't a good start. And now she's got a twin sister seventy-five miles east. It's a hard life, especially for women," he said, and looked at Mrs. Edgerton, who frowned at him. He tipped his hat to her before continuing. "I'm sorry to report, ma'am, that she's a place where decent women stay home."

Mrs. Edgerton turned toward him at that and said something quietly to her husband, who said, "Why is that, Mr. Plummer?" Henry smiled inside again, wondering whether the woman was shy, or too swollen up with pride to ask him herself.

"Ma'am, decent women stay home because they might get shot if they don't," he said, purposely being blunt, but honest. Hiding the truth wouldn't serve to help them once they got there. Mrs. Edgerton's posture stiffened while she looked straight ahead. "When someone is shot," he said, to remove any doubt of such a possibility, and thinking of Jack Cleveland, "a miner's court decides whether it's murder or self-defense. If it's murder, the court passes sentence, just like in the States. Either they're banished from the camp, or my duty is to hang them by the neck until they're dead. And I do my duty."

"Sheriff, must you be so frank?" Edgerton asked.

"Yes, sir, I must. If I'm not, when you get there, you'll wish I had been."

"Hmm," Edgerton said, "I see your point."

"If you don't now, you will when you get there," Henry said.

"What else should we know?" Edgerton said.

"That some no-accounts arrived in town not too long ago. I know them from California, and they're not to be trusted. They haven't done anything yet that I know of, but they will. I'm glad that more law-abiding citizens like you are coming in. Maybe when outlaws get wind of a Chief Justice in town, they'll pull foot to get out of town."

"You flatter me, Sheriff," Edgerton said. "I know better than to expect my presence to instill instant fear in such rambunctious men."

Henry grinned, and said, "That's a sad fact, your Honor. They'll not respect you any more than they do me."

Changing the subject, Sanders said, "Why did your wife leave for the States, Mr. Plummer?" Henry hesitated long enough to make Sanders wonder whether he would answer.

"Like I said, Sanders, life is hard out here, harder for women than men know. Rumors are as cruel as those who tell them, so I'll tell you the truth. My wife has gone East to be with family because my responsibilities have kept me away from home too often. If any man says otherwise, he'll answer to me." Henry spurred his horse and rode at the head of the party. He reckoned that other reasons were none of his business.

The days seemed long to Henry without Electa. His mood grew to match the gray clouds that came in from the north. He grew more distant as every day took her further away. Finally, after almost a week of traveling, he recognized the sagebrush flat that lay just south of the small valley that hid East Bannock, and before long they topped a hill and could look down on the wilderness community. Low clouds concealed the surrounding mountain peaks and added to the gloominess of the bleak, cold scene.

"The first row of buildings is Yankee Flat," Henry said, "for obvious reasons."

The women looked at one another with evident despair. One of Edgerton's young sons expressed everyone's first impression by saying, "I fink Bang Up is humbug." Henry heard the boy's remark and noticed the weary traveler's fallen expressions.

"Mr. Chief Justice, sir," Henry said, "I don't know what you expected, and it doesn't matter. She is what she is, an oasis in the wilderness." With that, he tipped his hat, nudged his horse to a trot, and rode ahead down the hill to Main Street, Chrisman's store, and his office.

Chapter Twenty Six ~ The Conspiracy

The two wagons of disheartened Bannock newcomers surveyed the quiet but dismal scene. Tanned hills splashed with the green-gray of sagebrush loomed before them, disappearing into low clouds. Log cabins as dark as coffee grounds released gray smoke into the vast, almost-winter dark skies, which was instantly dispersed by a cool wind. Lucia Darling, dark-haired and demure, had school teaching in common with Electa, though neither one knew it, since they had only made a brief acquaintance. Lucia looked across the small valley to a gallows and said, "Uncle Sidney, look," and pointed at the simple yet deadly sticks of timber, constructed to hang men.

"By the heavens, a gallows," he said. "The law has preceded us. But what kind of law remains to be seen. And, I see no steeple declaring that a prophet is here."

"I did expect to see a church steeple," Sanders said, "but now that we're here, I clearly expected too much. It's a most disappointing and unattractive place."

"True enough," Edgerton said, "but there is nowhere else to go for now. We must make the best of it. Fortunes are to be made in a place such as this. Well, let's find shelter before the north wind gets any colder." He snapped the reins and Sanders's wagon followed his, down the hill toward town. As they approached, they could hear water falling off the mountainside from the miner's sluice boxes.

Edgerton and Sanders checked their families into the Goodrich Hotel until houses could be found. That first night, the girls' spirits were so low that Mary, without her husband's knowledge, encouraged them with a promise that they would leave as soon as possible in the spring. Edgerton found a house for his family on their second day in Bannock.

"Mary, Plummer has sold me a house at a Sheriff's sale," he said. "It's only one room, but large enough."

"Do you mean as a permanent home here?" she said, fearing a lengthy stay.

"Today is the last day of September, my dear," he said, "and winter will soon be upon us. I do not intend to make others rich by renting rooms from them. We'll have our own house, such as it is. I don't intend to give anyone the impression that I'm a traveling peddler."

Sanders had to settle for a smaller house, which happened to be next door to the Vails. He was convinced that his influence and fortune would grow simultaneously with his Uncle Sidney's. He served as a sort of secretary, running errands for him as necessary.

The women set up housekeeping, hanging sheets on the walls to brighten the place. Both Mary Edgerton and Hattie Sanders were impressed with how quiet and orderly Bannock was. Mary, unlike Martha and Electa, was indignant to live in such close proximity to "wild Indians," who begged for food and peeked in her windows whenever they wanted. In the ensuing weeks, Martha worried incessantly about Electa. Her loneliness matched that of Electa's, when she came to realize that the only close neighbors either the Sanders's or the Edgerton's wanted was each other.

While the new families got settled in, Henry and his deputies kept busy patrolling Bannock and Virginia City, as the newest strike had come to be called, although some continued to call it Alder Gulch, and the road between them. For several weeks, Edgerton and his nephew Sanders frequented the saloons and businesses so they could acquaint themselves with the men of the area. They particularly wanted to investigate the political condition of the towns and discover who, besides Sheriff Plummer, was influential, and in what ways. One evening after dark, Sanders went to Edgerton's home to report as usual, and knocked on the door, which Mary opened.

"Good evening, Mary," he said as he entered, his hat in hand.

"Good evening, Wilbur," she replied. "Come in and have a cup of coffee. Uncle Sidney is waiting for you."

"Hello, my boy," Edgerton said. "The coffee will wait. I'll get my coat, and we'll go for a walk."

"Yes, sir," Sanders said.

"May I go with you, sir?" Henry Tilden asked. As Edgerton's ward, he looked up to the Chief Justice and spent as much time with him as possible.

"No, my boy, it's too cold for you tonight. You'd best remain here," Edgerton said.

Sanders opened the door for his uncle and they left. The men waited until they were away from the house and alone before speaking.

"Have you heard that the Peabody Stage was robbed near the Rattlesnake Ranch?" Sanders said.

"Yes, an inevitable event," Edgerton said stopping to light a cigar. "But one that will eventually turn to our advantage. All right, Wilbur, tell me what you've learned."

"As we thought," Sanders said beginning to walk again, "the Masons are the most influential organization, notwithstanding the Union League and the Miner's Union. Plummer was active in those two, but quit the League. He had applied for membership in the Mason's, but was rejected. I suspicion he was refused based on his questionable past. But the people are no doubt behind him, or he would never have been elected."

"I'm certain you're right on each count," Edgerton said. "A man in his position is powerful, and might yet be appointed as deputy marshal. He's got over half his term yet to serve and is no man's puppet. He is highly respected. We must not underestimate him, nor can we trust him. He's the acknowledged civil magnate of the entire country for now, but when the time is right, we'll have him removed as any possible threat. In the meantime, I'll make a declaration that the name of Bannock has been officially changed to Bannack, which will serve to at least begin to establish my authority as Chief Justice."

They reached the end of the sidewalk, crossed the street, and continued back down the other side. A harvest moon shone scattered snow on the street, sidewalks, rooftops, and the surrounding hills.

"Shouldn't we have gone to Lewiston so you could be sworn in?" Sanders said.

"No, there is no need for that. The President himself appointed me, and I'll not allow my commission to be jeopardized by a ruffian with a tarnished reputation. Or by any organization, for that matter. We'll use them instead to our ends. I'll appear at every trial, take every opportunity to speak publicly, and introduce new legislation at the appropriate time. As far as I'm concerned, in this wilderness, my authority follows me as Chief Justice. And I'll be hornswaggled if I'll allow anyone to undermine that authority, including Plummer, sheriff or not."

"But Uncle Sidney, how do you propose to get control?"

"Crime is our opportunity. Since there has been one stage robbery, there will be others. Sheriff Plummer left town as soon as he heard of it, and hasn't been seen since."

"But what do stage robberies have to do with us?" Sanders said.

"The citizenry will go the whole hog to end such carryings-on by ruffians. We'll give Plummer a little time to catch the thieves, but if he fails, as he undoubtedly will, vigilante justice will step in."

"Uncle!" Sanders exclaimed. "Vigilantes!"

"Quiet, my boy, get hold of yourself. Surely you don't expect to rise to prominence and wealth in a land of opportunity such as this, without manipulating a few circumstances. What do you think politics is all about, pretty speeches to pretty girls? It would be helpful if the most influential men were Masons, but it's not necessary. Influence is what counts, my boy. Rank isn't everything. Remember that."

"Yes, sir," Sanders said. "Well, Paris Pfouts and James Williams come to mind. When will we, I mean, how will we start such a movement?"

"First, we'll wait. The right time must present itself. This is big country, and the sheriff and his few deputies have little chance of catching disguised road agents. When the time is right, we'll approach Mr. Pfouts and Mr. Williams about accomplishing what inept lawmen cannot. Until then, we'll spread doubt about the good sheriff's character."

Sanders nodded his understanding. They had returned to the Edgerton residence, where they went inside for a cup of Mary's hot coffee.

~

As October ended and November began, the two men invested in several mines and bought a small herd of cattle. They also executed their plan to lodge doubt about Henry's integrity in the minds of Bannack's citizens. They attacked his suspicious past by paying men to spread word of his prison record, and debated the doubtful reputation of a man whose wife would leave him.

Of course, word eventually got back to Henry. Although keenly aware that the events of his life were taking a turn for the worse, Henry was more depressed about Electa leaving than he was concerned about the slander. Since he wouldn't have smeared another man's name, he didn't spend any time wondering about whom to suspect. He reckoned, as Electa had said, that chickens come home to roost sooner or later, and that words do the same. He also reckoned that tried friends were true friends, like Joseph, and perhaps Francis Thompson.

Henry liked Francis, but felt that he didn't know shucks about judging men. He had unwittingly guided a band of outlaws to Bannock. Henry suspected that he had told them about shipments of goods he had ordered. Feeling sorry for the inexperienced proprietor, Henry went to Francis's store to warn him, and found him stocking shelves with goods.

"Thompson," Henry said, "I've been watching those men you made friends with on the trail from Cottonwood. As I said before, that was a mistake, so don't make another one."

"What are you talking about?" Francis said as he worked.

"They've been keeping an eye on your store. Are you expecting something?" Henry said.

"A big shipment from Salt Lake City is on the trail."

"Did you tell them when it would be coming?"

"I might have," Francis said defensively. "In fact, I believe I did. What business is it of yours?"

"My business is to make your business safe, Thompson. If you'll take my advice, you'll not open that door after dark, if the knocker is one of the men you brought to town. When your freight arrives, I'll help you unload and stack it to protect everything else inside, including you. I suggest that you continue to sleep here and keep a gun loaded while you're at it. I'll see you later at the Vails for supper." Henry turned to leave, but stopped as Francis spoke again.

"Of course you're right, Henry," Francis said. "I believe you know your business, and you know men probably better than I ever will. I apologize for flying at you like that. I'm much obliged to you for offering your help, and I know Joseph will appreciate it too."

"Don't mention it. Just keep your trap shut and we'll all sleep better at night," Henry said, grinning.

~

While keeping an eye on the Thompson-Swift store over the next few weeks, Henry noticed that Edgerton spent an increasing amount of time there, visiting with Francis. Henry, Francis, and Joseph continued to take their meals with the Vails. Joseph and Henry remained on the best of terms, as the young man looked up to Henry almost as a big brother. But Henry began to detect a certain uneasiness about Francis, and he suspected that it came from Edgerton.

On a cold evening in early November, Henry noticed Joseph coming out of a hurdy gurdy house on Main Street. The young man nervously looked around when he came out, started across the street, saw Henry approaching him, turned on his heels, and went back inside the gambling house in a vain attempt to avoid his good friend.

"Whoa, there, pardner," Henry said stopping him just inside the door by placing a hand on his shoulder.

"Oh, hello, Henry. Nice meal Martha had for us this evening, don't you reckon?" Joseph said nervously.

"I do," Henry said putting an arm around his shoulders. "Say, Joe," he said, turning the young man around, and leading him back outside, "this is no place for you."

"I reckon you're right about that, Henry," he said, his hands in his pockets while ashamedly kicking at the sidewalk with his toe.

"You're making good money with Francis at the store, aren't you?" Henry said.

"Why, sure enough," Joseph said with a grin.

"Then why not use the sense God gave a goose, and hold onto it? Gambling is a fast way to become a poor man."

"Much obliged, Henry," Joseph said. "See you at breakfast." Henry tipped his hat to his young friend, who headed toward the east end of town and the Vails.

~

Early one morning In mid November, Edgerton had an errand in mind for Tilden. He thought the boy old enough for more responsibility. He assigned the task at breakfast.

"Young man," Edgerton said, "Wilbur and I have decided that you're ready for a job more befitting a young man your age. After all, you turned fifteen this summer."

"Excited, Tilden looked at Mary for her approval. She smiled and nodded, encouraging him.

"Thank you, sir," Tilden said. "What would you like me to do?"

"I'd like you to take that red gelding of Wilbur's that you're so fond of and ride south and west of here to Horse Prairie as soon as you're finished with breakfast. Mrs. Edgerton has packed you a dinner to take along." Mary smiled and placed the package next to his plate.

"Do you remember where the pasture is? Where we took the cattle last month?"

"Yes, sir, it's like you said, south and west of here. Out on the expanse."

"That's right. Out on the expanse. Find as many of our cattle as you can, and push them back here. Leave them outside of town, find Wilbur, and tell him that you're back. We'll expect you before nightfall."

"Yes, sir," Tilden said, and did as he was told, as usual.

~

That same day, Sheriff Plummer led an outfit of riders north and west to Rattlesnake Ranch to look after a herd of horses for Frank Parrish, who was so sick that Plummer reckoned that the man would die. Edgerton, however, assumed that they were going somewhere to prospect for silver, for which the sheriff had a definite skill, and sent Sanders after them on a mule, the only mode of four-legged transportation available.

It took Tilden half the morning to reach Horse Prairie, and longer to find the cattle than anyone reckoned it would. The animals gave him more trouble than he imagined they could. They were more like wild deer than livestock. He chased them for the rest of the day in the general direction toward Bannack. The sun sank below the western mountains, leaving only an orange glow above them. He wondered if he was in trouble for being so late, but felt so tired that he didn't much care. Hoarse from hollering at the animals, he forced them along toward Bannack through the increasing darkness.

Suddenly, nearby noises startled him. He reined his horse up, surprised to see three horsemen emerge from the darkness of a ravine and ride toward him. He wondered who they were, and what they might want with him. "Maybe they're going to Bannack, and will help me take the untamed beasts the rest of the way," he thought. As they got closer he was confused because he couldn't see their faces. All three wore hats, long coats, masks; and cloth hoods over their heads with round eyeholes cut out with a slit at the mouth. The strange-looking men reined their horses up, seemingly surrounding him.

"Whoa up, there," one of them said with a muffled voice.

"Yes, sir, what do you want?" Tilden said.

"Shut your trap, boy!" the same voice barked. The man spurred his horse and rode right up next to him. Tilden became too scared to move.

"Get your hands, up, boy," he said and Tilden did that, too. The road agent roughly patted him down, slapping his coat pockets. "Empty your pockets." Tilden obeyed, retrieving a simple comb and a likeness of his girl. "I told you he's just a boy. And boys don't carry gold or cash," the man said, and spurred his horse back toward the ravine. The others followed without saying a word.

Relief weakened Tilden's legs and met the fear in his chest at his stomach. As the barely visible men disappeared back down into the ravine, he spurred the tired horse on until the lights of Bannack shined below him. Suddenly the gelding stumbled, and fell hard into a ditch. Frightened, Tilden yelled as he went down, but fell clear of the horse. Stunned, he lay in the dirt between clumps of sagebrush. After awhile, he didn't know how long, he came to himself, shook his head, gathered himself up, saw the lights of Bannack, and began to run. Yelling, running, tripping over sagebrush in the dark, falling again and yet again, still yelling as he descended the hill. Hattie Sanders had stepped behind the house for some fresh air when she heard him. Exhausted, Tilden stumbled across Yankee Flat right to where Hattie stood.

"Three men," Tilden said and collapsed to his knees at her feet.

"Why, Henry Tilden!" she exclaimed. Putting her arm around his waist, she helped him into the house. The fresh smell of sagebrush was on his coat.

"Wilbur has gone to Alder Gulch. Sit here by the fire while I get you some coffee," she said.

Finally, he got his breath and took a sip of coffee. Dirty from his long day of labor, his hair unkempt, he wiped his wet brow with a sleeve before speaking.

"I was an hour away, on the other side of Horse Prairie Hill," Tilden said. "Three men tried to rob me, but I didn't have anything they wanted. Road agents, I reckon." Hattie sat down, dismayed at hearing such news. "And Mrs. Sanders," Tilden said, "one of the men I know was Sheriff Plummer."

Chapter Twenty Seven ~ Crime, Character, and Consequences

"Sheriff Plummer!" Hattie whispered. "Are you certain?"

"Well, I reckon so. I recognized his overcoat," Tilden said defensively.

"His overcoat? Didn't you see his face?"

"No, they all had hoods on," Tilden said. "But the one had a coat like the sheriff's."

But this time of year," Hattie said, "everyone wears an overcoat."

"But the sheriff's has a red lining," Tilden said, "and so did the man's."

Hattie sighed. "Henry, I don't doubt that you were robbed, or rather, that three men tried to rob you, but, how can you be sure that one of them was Sheriff Plummer, when you couldn't see his face? I really don't think that the sheriff," she said, but Tilden interrupted.

"I just know that I saw the sheriff's coat that has a red lining. I've got to get to the Edgerton's. I'm already late, Mrs. Sanders. Thank you for the coffee. I feel better now." He got up to leave.

"I'll get my coat and go with you," Hattie said. At the Edgerton's, Mattie, Lucia and Mary were sitting at the table around a lone oil lamp darning socks and talking when Tilden opened the door for Mrs. Sanders. She entered and stepped aside so the Edgertons could see that Tilden was with her. Sidney, reading by firelight in a simple chair, looked up when they entered the house. Though Tilden had caught his breath, he was still a disheveled sight.

"Henry!" Edgerton said surprised at his appearance. "What's wrong?"

"Wilbur," Hattie said, "Henry was robbed by three men."

"Sit down, boy," Edgerton said, "and tell me what happened."

Tilden recounted his tale from beginning to end, up until the time he had arrived at the Sanders's. He again ended his story by saying again, "One of the men I know was Henry Plummer."

Edgerton questioned him as Hattie had, and Tilden repeated the same answers, so Edgerton told him to sleep on it. The following day, Sanders returned from Rattlesnake Ranch on the mule, unsuccessful in his search for the sheriff. Hattie related the news to him and said, "Sidney wants to see you right away." Edgerton had Tilden repeat his story once again for Wilbur. Mary, Lucia and Mattie listened intently while quietly preparing supper.

"How dark was it?" Sanders said.

"That's a fool question, Wilbur," Edgerton said. "How is the boy going to explain that?" He turned again to Tilden.

"Son," he said, though he wasn't his son, "how far away were they when you first saw them coming toward you?" Tilden thought about the question before answering.

"Oh, one hundred fifty feet, I should say," he said.

"And they rode right up to you," Sanders said.

"No, sir, just the one who felt my clothes and told me to empty my pockets."

"Then, how far away was the one you believe was the sheriff?" Edgerton said.

"Ten feet or so, no more than fifteen."

"Hmm," Edgerton said, considering his answer. "And what makes you think that Plummer was one of the men?"

"Because he had on that overcoat of his he always wears, lined with red."

"The overcoat is convincing," Wilbur said. "No one else in town has one like it." He turned to the women who had stopped working and simply stood there listening, and said, "Girls, never breathe a word of what you have heard, or our lives will not be safe." Mattie gasped as the women looked at each other with large, frightened eyes.

"Come, Wilbur," Edgerton said, "Let's go to town. Thank you, young man." After they had crossed the footbridge, Edgerton glanced around to make certain no one could hear. "No one else in town has an overcoat like the sheriff's *that we know of.* You know as well as I do, that there was only a mere sliver of a moon last night, and clouds besides. That means very little light, if any, to see by, even at ten feet."

"Yes, sir, that it was a black night is true enough," Sanders said.

"True enough to relieve any incriminating charges concerning Sheriff Plummer," Edgerton said. "But there is enough fuel to add to the fire. And soon, we will organize a force of vigilantes." Sanders nodded his understanding.

~

The next day, the sheriff heard about the holdup and went directly to the Bannack Express Office, where Tilden worked, to talk to him about it. The youngster had the sheriff's guilt so set in his mind that fear gripped him as soon as he saw the lawman cross the street toward the office. Plummer's health had only deteriorated since Electa's leaving. His complexion had paled, and his features softened from their former tough ruddiness to a nearly effeminate appearance. His almost constant traveling In the cold had worsened his cough until it became a persistent trait of the man. Still, the sheriff's position, reputation, and Tilden's own alleged lawless encounter frightened him.

"Henry, I hear tell you had some excitement," Plummer said shutting the door. He clapped and rubbed his gloved hands together to warm them.

"Yes, sir, I reckon you could call it that," Tilden replied from behind the wooden counter. The Sheriff walked right up to it and looked him straight in the eye.

"Well, did you recognize any of them?" Tilden hesitated.

"No, sir, I sure didn't," he finally said, sighing.

"I hear tell they wore hoods, but was there anything about them or their horses that could help me find them? Their voices?"

"No, sir, it was darker than the inside of a cow, and only one of them said anything, and I didn't recognize his voice." Disgusted, the sheriff gently pounded the countertop with his fist.

"Well," Plummer said, "if you think of anything, let me know. If I catch them, they'll spend a time in my jail until they hang for certain sure." He thanked Tilden anyway, and left, coughing as he entered the cold outside air.

~

Several days later, three hooded road agents came out of the cold darkness between Bannack and Virginia City and robbed the Oliver Stage. It only had two passengers, but the thieves got one hundred dollars in treasury notes, and four hundred dollars in gold. The robberies became the talk of both Bannack and Virginia City.

Francis noticed that Henry had been out of Bannack during both stage holdups, as well as for the attempted robbery of Henry Tilden. That coincidence added credibility to the stories he had heard at the Goodrich Saloon, and those that Edgerton told him even at his own store. As a result, Martha's meals became awkward and unpleasant for Francis, who felt increasingly ill at ease around the sheriff. Plummer sensed something odd, but couldn't put his finger on anything definite. The thought that Francis was a road agent was outlandish, since the man could hardly ride a horse.

Tilden's informal testimony of Plummer's alleged lawlessness intrigued Mattie Edgerton, but she didn't suspect his story to be fact. According to Sidney, rumors about the sheriff were all over town. The Sunday before Thanksgiving, Edgerton went to Francis's store on one of his many visits. Francis saw him coming, opened the door for the chief justice, and then surprised him by locking it as soon as he was inside.

"Judge," Francis said insistently, "who is doing this robbing?" Edgerton took his hat and coat off, set them on a barrel, and looked at him.

"I don't know that I should make my opinion known," Edgerton said. "But, since you're a leading businessman, a trusted friend, and his friend, I suppose you should know."

"His friend?" Francis said. "Who? What are you talking about?"

"Sheriff Henry Plummer," Edgerton said.

"Plummer! Are you serious? I've heard rumors, but," Francis said sitting down on a crate.

"My ward, Henry Tilden, recognized the sheriff as one of the men who tried to rob him."

"What do you mean, he recognized him? Plummer wouldn't ride up to someone, even a boy, and rob them if he could be recognized."

"The men wore hoods, but Tilden recognized his coat. It's the only one in town with a red lining," Edgerton said. Francis thought for a moment.

"That's pretty slim," Francis said, "but I've been wondering about him myself. As you know, he takes his meals with us at the Vails." He hesitated again and looked at the judge. "Plummer's been out of town during both stage robberies and Tilden's."

"There is something else," Edgerton said. "You know that I've been planning a trip to Washington D. C.. "Plummer told me that he frequently sends money to his widowed mother, and he has asked me exactly when I'm leaving. He wants me to take his money along, and send it on to his mother at my convenience. Francis, I just wonder if I'm being set up for a robbery. Well, if I had any doubts, I don't now. Blast it all! Mary has accepted the Vail's invitation to Thanksgiving dinner, which Plummer will no doubt attend."

"I, too, have told Martha that I'll be there," Francis said. Troubled, he stood up and unlocked the door.

"I believe," Edgerton said putting his coat and hat on, "that I'd better postpone my travels until something can be done to make things quite a bit safer around here." He said good bye and left.

~

Henry Plummer insisted on paying for almost the entire Thanksgiving dinner. He bought beef from the Stuart brother's new butcher shop, and ordered a forty pound turkey from Salt Lake City that cost him one dollar per pound. He also ordered one dozen bottles of fine California wine, and gave Martha money enough to buy potatoes, real butter, cider for the children, and fixings for cheesecake and everything else.

Mattie, Mary, and Lucia got up early on Thanksgiving to cook the elaborate meal. It took a long morning to prepare Boston baked beans, Boston brown bread, egg-nog, and Indian pudding, not to mention cranberry sauce, a variety of meats, pickles, pastries, rolls, and desserts. The Edgerton family walked to the Vails in the November cold under a clear sky more blue than Hattie thought sky could be. She said, "The Vails haven't been the most admired family in town until today. I imagine that everyone in town should want to enjoy this dinner."

Some two dozen guests arrived at the Vails just before noon to enjoy the finest and what would be the most talked about meal in Bannack history. Both the turkey and the wines were popular by everyone but Mary and Wilbur, who insisted on abstaining.

It was dark when the Edgerton's walked home that evening. "That was the most memorable meal this town shall probably ever witness," Hattie said. "It was one of the most splendid dinners I ever attended. Everything that money could buy was served."

"Yes," Lucia agreed, "it was marvelous. Sheriff Plummer is a most able host."

"How would you describe the good sheriff, Hattie?" Edgerton said. She looked back toward the Vail's house before answering.

"I would describe him as slender, graceful, and mild of speech. He has pleasing manners and fine address, a fair complexion, sandy hair and blue eyes; the last person whom one would select as something other than what he represents himself to be."

"I see," Edgerton said. "And as a woman, I assume you have given his separation from his wife some consideration. How do you account for such a state of affairs?"

"I asked Mrs. Vail about her sister, Mrs. Plummer," Hattie said, "and I have come to believe that she is a splendid Christian woman. I suspicion that Mr. Plummer sent her away because he felt that he was not fit to live with her. I also believe him to be a sincere man, which is very likely his finest trait."

"I would imagine," Mary said, "that they miss one another very much."

In fact, Electa regretted leaving her husband, and missed Henry more than she did the Vails. Henry went on and did his job as though he were destined to.

~

For the next two weeks, he did what he had to do, and more. He levied fines, searched for road agents, found lost cattle and horses, and continued patrolling Bannack, Virginia City, and the road between, along with his deputies. He did it all from duty, and with a heavy heart. He knew most of the men in the country. He respected their right to work without interference from him or anyone else. He also felt that it was his duty to protect them and their property while they worked, and to keep an eye on those who felt that their business was to steal the property of others.

Known as a trusted confidant, the sheriff often heard of impending gold shipments. Few shipments had been taken by stage since the two robberies. Gold dust was either cleverly hidden in freight wagons, or taken to Salt Lake City or Fort Benton by one or two men. Consequently, when he heard that John Largent and Matt Carroll were about to take gold dust to Fort Benton by way of Bannack, he found them in Virginia City and asked them when they planned to leave. He had already decided to follow them to make sure they got through safely.

"Well, Sheriff," Largent said, nervously looking at Carroll, "we plan to leave in a couple days on the seventeenth. But we didn't know our plans were all over town."

Plummer grinned and said, "I don't know that they are. Maybe I'll see you on the trail."

That made them nervous. Unfortunately, like most everyone else, they had heard the stories suspecting him of being a road agent. Plummer waited for Largent and Carroll to leave Virginia City and then followed them at a distance. He didn't know how they carried the dust, but that didn't matter. He only knew that they had it, and that he must give them protection.

The two men reached Dempsey's Ranch by nightfall. Plummer showed up later, under the pretense that he was looking for a pair of stray horses. Of course, all of the men were well armed. Largent and Carroll expected trouble to come from the sheriff. The duo bid Sheriff Plummer goodbye after breakfast the next morning, and left him to search for the horses. They reached Point of Rocks that night, a landmark by the Beaverhead River halfway to Bannack, and found Plummer already there. The whispered stories came to mind when they saw him, and their fears grew. The sheriff, as friendly as ever, had the men puzzled. Rather than making a move for their gold, and daring any violence against them, he seemed more like an escort.

"Any sign of those horses yet, sheriff?" Largent said around the breakfast fire.

"Not yet," Plummer said. "I believe I'll look as far west as Bannack, though. They might have gone that far."

"We were wishin' that we had a place to sleep inside tonight at Bannack," Carroll said. "Maybe you know of a place that wouldn't charge us very much, sheriff?"

Henry grinned at the suggestion. "You gents go to the Thompson-Swift store and tell Mr. Thompson that I said that he can put you up for the night. I'll be along directly, and sleep there myself tonight."

"Much obliged, sheriff," Largent said, looking at Carroll, who nodded in agreement.

The men split up again. Sheriff Plummer lagged behind and looked for the horses while the men went on to Bannack. They hadn't told him where they kept their gold, but he didn't care, since he didn't need to know. He arrived in Bannack that evening, after Francis had closed the store and just as the men spread their blankets on the floor. He chatted with Francis for a few minutes, spread his blanket on the counter, and went to sleep. A cold morning met them. Plummer led them through a skiff of snow to Martha's for a hot breakfast, where they were more than welcome.

"Gentlemen," Henry said at breakfast, "I believe I've passed those wild ponies somewhere on the trail. I'll just mosey back in the direction of Alder Gulch and see if I can't come across them. I would advise you to make camp at the Big Hole River crossing. It's a good day's ride from here, and tomorrow you can make Deer Lodge."

"We want to make Fort Benton by Christmas, so we're much obliged to you a second time," Largent said.

"A second time?" James said sipping his coffee.

"Sheriff Plummer made the way clear for us to sleep at Thompson's store," Carroll said grinning.

"Henry has been known to do people favors," Martha said, picking up dishes.

Largent and Carroll remained unconvinced of the sheriff's humanitarian efforts. Their fear got the better of them, and after the day's ride they chose to hide from him by camping in the brush, rather than take his advice. They didn't see the sheriff the next night at Deer Lodge, or the next two nights either, which they spent at ranches, so they assumed he had returned to Alder Gulch. Each night was colder than the last. They finally arrived safely at Fort Benton on Christmas Eve. There, one of the first men they came across was Sheriff Henry Plummer.

"Hello, gents," Henry said as they entered the general store, surprising them.

"Why, hello, sheriff," Largent said. "What brings you to Fort Benton in this weather?"

"I had to make sure a gold shipment made it through. You understand," he said, grinning. Wide-eyed, the men looked at each other. They understood that he meant their gold, and that he had suffered much cold discomfort over many miles to make certain that they weren't troubled on the trail. They also understood that the rumors about him were nothing more than whispered stories.

Chapter Twenty Eight ~ Vigilante Justice

While Sheriff Plummer had been escorting Largent and Carroll's gold to Fort Benton, a crime far worse than attempted robbery had taken place near Alder Gulch. A young German man, Nicholas Tbalt, was found, murdered. He had been missing for over a week, when a grouse hunter followed a downed bird to his body. It happened to lie on a ranch belonging to a suspected road agent, George Ives.

Nicholas Tbalt had gone to George Ives's ranch to fetch a mule team. The young man had disappeared, and without Ives's knowledge, his body had been found and taken by wagon to Virginia City. The citizens there became furious at the discovery that a rope burn graced Tbalt's neck. His frozen hand clutched the leavings of sagebrush, obviously evidence that he had been hauled through the brush while still alive.

George Ives, tall and blonde, could ride a horse like a Blackfoot Indian. The loose women in Virginia City liked him. The proprietors of the town didn't care to see him coming, since he had the uncivilized habit of leading his horse into every business he frequented, which made a mess of things. For his honest money, Ives boarded the animals that pulled the supply trains in from Salt Lake City.

When Ives's name came to the forefront of suspects, Sanders recalled that Sheriff Plummer had said that he suspected Ives of robbing the Oliver Stage. Upon being accused of killing Tbalt for gold dust, Alder Gulch citizens took him into custody, and Sanders saw his opportunity. The week before Christmas, Edgerton had sent Sanders to the Gulch to drum up support for a new territory in eastern Idaho. Of course, Edgerton hoped to be appointed as its governor.

Most miners weren't very busy in late December. They had plenty of time to attend a murder trial. Sanders joined a crowd in Nevada City, one of a string of small communities in Alder

Gulch, to view the body. The thought occurred to him that he should offer to prosecute whoever might stand accused. In Sanders's mind, it all came together and made sense.

"Men," he said, addressing the crowd on the snowy street, "this is a struggle between good and evil, law and lawlessness. I hereby volunteer my services as a prosecuting attorney to your fair community. Believe me when I say that if there is no law and order, there will be order without law." Few knew what he meant by that, but the crowd cheered his short but effective speech anyway. That was the last time most of them liked what he had to say, since, like most lawyers and preachers, he turned out to be long-winded.

Two empty freight wagons served as a sort of outdoor court, one for the defense and the other for the prosecution. A bonfire was built to ward off the cold, and benches situated in a semicircle around it for the jury. A Judge Byham presided. A portly gentleman, he shaved only his upper lip and the front of his chin.

The defense attorney sent a man named George Lane to Bannack to tell Plummer about the unauthorized arrest of Ives and the trial. Lane went gladly, since Plummer had helped him with mining concerns a number of times. It took him two days to reach Bannack with the news. He found Sheriff Plummer in his office in the back of Chrisman's store and explained the situation to him.

"Sheriff, I've said what I came to say," George said, "but I heard mention that you shouldn't show up in Alder." From what I heard tell, I don't reckon you should go. There's talk that you're behind the holdups. Some want to hang you and your deputies." Henry chuckled at the notion.

"Well, I don't reckon that even Sanders would try to hang me, at least not without his uncle to back him up," Plummer said. "Besides, the trial started two days ago and is probably over and done with by now. If not, it soon will be. Sanders started this party. I reckon he can finish it."

About a thousand people attended the three-day trial at one time or another. Ives, wearing his buffalo coat, sat shackled in the defense wagon on a box. Finally one dissenting juror prevented a unanimous verdict, but Sanders would have none of it. He jumped up into the witness wagon and raised his arms to the crowd.

"Citizens of Alder!" he cried. "I make a motion that the lone opposing vote be ignored and the majority vote of this lawful jury be accepted as the will of the people!"

"I second the motion!" a voice said quickly from the crowd.

"I also move," Sanders continued now that he had the crowd's attention, "that George Ives be hanged immediately!" The crowd stood to its feet in the snow, shouting, clapping, and stomping, as much to keep warm as to demonstrate their approval. More than one voice seconded the new motion.

Ives slowly shuffled his chained feet over to Sanders and shook his hand. The crowd hushed to hear what either would say.

"Sanders, could my end be put off until morning?" Ives said.

Before Sanders could say a word, a short rotund guard named X. Beidler, holding a shotgun and sitting on his haunches on a nearby rooftop, said, "Sanders, ask him how long he gave the Dutchman!" Rudely, Sanders ignored the condemned man's request and made yet a third motion.

"I also move that the court take possession of the property of George Ives to pay the expenses of his trial!"

A chorus of angry voices rose again in agreement. Judge Byham stepped down from the wagon and stood by Ives. The afternoon sun's power had faded. Shadows had appeared while the jury convened, and the temperature began to drop quickly.

"Let's get on with it," the judge said. "The sun's going down and the fire's going out! Sanders, have you any suggestions as to where the execution shall take place?"

"Right there in that house," X. Beidler said from his perch. "There's no roof on it yet, but the main beam is strong enough for a rope." Sanders walked over to the unfinished building, looked inside, and nodded at the judge, who took Ives by the arm and led him before six armed men into the building. Sanders directed one of the guards to set a dry goods box on its side below the main beam. Two other guards set their weapons aside and helped Ives step up onto the box. The rope's length was adjusted and tied off.

"George Ives, have you anything to say before you are hung for the murder of Nicholas Tbalt?" Sanders said.

George looked around him at the crowd who had swarmed into the place and those that spilled out into the snow-covered street to watch him die and said, "I am innocent of this crime; Alex Carter killed the Dutchman." Sanders's face reddened as he and Judge Byham looked at one another. The judge nodded at a guard standing behind Ives, who kicked the wooden box out from under him.

Even before Ives stopped swaying, Sanders moved deliberately through the crowd to several specific men and whispered something to each one. The first two went outside and up the street, and the last man followed Sanders out. There, he approached two more. They, too, immediately left the crowd. Darkness had fallen quickly on the December night. All six men went either directly or indirectly to the Lott brother's store. In an alley behind the store, Sanders quietly entered through the door, lit a lamp, and shook hands with each man as he went in. They formed a semicircle in front of him.

"Gentlemen," Sanders said, "you all heard the murderer name one of his accomplices. God only knows how many more murderers and road agents are about. It should be obvious to every thinking Jack of a man, that the sheriff is incompetent and unable to capture even one road agent." The men nodded in agreement. "Also," Sanders continued, "as a prosecutor whose uncle is the chief justice of the territory, let me assure you that prosecuting every last rogue is going to be extremely slow, not to mention expensive. They must be found out, chased down, and brought to justice. Therefore, I assume that you all consent to our proposal to form a Citizens Vigilante Committee."

The men all nodded their agreement.

"Raise your right hand and repeat after me," Sanders said, and the men obeyed him. "I swear to be true to each member of the Citizen's Vigilant Committee, to reveal no secrets, and to violate no laws of right. I swear to never reveal, as long as I live, the name of any member of the Committee." The men dropped their hands and several of them sighed. Gentlemen, be back here at eight o'clock in the morning with at least one other man who can be trusted. You're going after Alex Carter."

~

The vigilantes, including X. Beidler, learned that Carter had gone to Deer Lodge Creek. But upon their arrival there after a week of cold late December travel, they were told that Carter had gone to the Cottonwood stage station. They pressed on, only to find that he had been warned of his imminent capture by a letter from Red Yeager, one of the men Francis Thompson had guided to Bannack and Plummer later warned Francis about. Yeager wasn't tall; less than five and a half feet, and thin, with blazing red hair and whiskers.

The secret posse pushed on through the snow, following the fugitive's tracks to Rattlesnake Ranch, near the Point of Rocks. Sheriff Plummer knew nothing of their mission or their movements. After two weeks in the cold with little relief or shelter, they apprehended their quarry. During their cold chase, New Year's Day had come and gone.

Yeager admitted to warning Carter, but blamed a rough named George Brown of writing the letter. The vigilantes arrested Brown too. Instead of going to Bannack, they took their prisoners to Laurin's ranch, a few miles north of Nevada City. They were allowed a few hours sleep and then awakened with an order to write down the name of every member of their gang.

Sitting on the floor in chains with his back against a log wall, Yeager grinned.

"You gents think you're big bugs," he said, "but I wasn't born in the woods to be scared by a passel of owls. Does the sheriff know what you're about?" The vigilantes just looked at one another. "I reckon he doesn't," Yeager said. "Well, I'm goin' to fix his flint." He wrote a name down and handed the paper to a vigilante, who looked at it and read, "Henry Plummer."

The self-appointed lawmen persevered in obtaining more names from Yeager. On January fourth they executed both him and George Brown from the limb of a cottonwood tree at Laurin's ranch.

The successful Citizen's Vigilante Committee rode the few miles through bitter cold to Alder Gulch and found more like-minded men who were sworn to secrecy and eager to pursue supposed road agents. The executive officers of the self-regulating committee adamantly sent four men, again including the now experienced X. Beidler, to Bannack to execute Sheriff Plummer and two of his deputies, Ned Ray and Buck Stinson.

Meanwhile, an alleged horse thief by the name of Dutch John had been caught and taken to Bannack by a private citizen, Neil Howie. Howie had heard of the vigilante hangings and took Dutch at gunpoint to Chrisman's store, where he found the sheriff.

"I see you brought me a prisoner," Plummer said when they walked in.

"Dutch is in my custody," Howie said. "Just wanted you to know. I've played the Devil to catch him, and I'm going to keep him."

"What's the charge against him?" Plummer said.

"He's a horse thief," Howie said.

"Well, I suppose you are willing that he should be tried by the civil authorities," Plummer said and coughed. Howie remained silent. "This new way our people have of hanging men without law or evidence isn't exactly the thing to do," Plummer said. "It's time a stop was put to it."

"Let's go, Dutch. Back outside," Howie said. Plummer followed them out front and watched as Howie marched his prisoner down Main Street towards the footbridge. Several men approached Howie and his prisoner. He explained his actions as well as what he had heard about the vigilantes. Plummer went back inside. Howie found an empty cabin on Yankee Flat, where he held his prisoner and waited for help from the vigilantes.

~

The next evening, Beidler and company arrived in Bannack. At the Goodrich Saloon they learned about Howie and his prisoner, but many residents were unsure about whether to support the vigilantes or not. Beidler, cold, tired, and disgusted, gave up trying to start a Bannack arm of the committee for the night.

~

Sanders had returned to Bannack and enjoyed the protection of armed guards for a week, paid for by the sale of George Ives's property. Since the vigilantes had organized, Sanders and Edgerton voiced their opinions and spoke openly of capturing the rest of the road agents, at least in Edgerton's house.

At home, Mattie and Mary worked on bread dough across the room, and the children played on a bed.

"Uncle Sidney," Sanders said sipping coffee at the table, "we could save the committee the trouble and attention of Plummer's public trial, as well as the expense, by secretly warning him of capture. He's certain to run, and when he goes to the stable for his horse, he can be shot for trying to escape justice."

"Hmm," Edgerton mused. He stoked the fire with a poker and placed more wood on it before he spoke. Sanders waited patiently, confident that his idea would work.

"No, I'm afraid that won't do, Wilbur," Edgerton said. Sanders looked puzzled.

"Because questions will be asked as to who placed the assassins at the stable, and who warned him of impending judgment. Besides, we both know that no point of law would support such action."

~

The evening of January ninth found James Vail out of town on business. Plummer hadn't been feeling well for almost a week, and Martha had insisted that he rest at their house. The Vail boarders, Joseph Swift and Francis Thompson, continued to take their meals with Martha, the children, and Henry, just like they had at Sun River Farm. That seemed a long time ago to Henry.

He had mixed feelings about Electa. He missed her terribly; more than he would have missed living if he were to die, but also felt glad that she wasn't there to see him. He felt like death warmed over, and reckoned that he looked like it. At times his coughing was so persistent that he became embarrassed, and left the room, or the table if they were eating. No one said anything about it, for which he was grateful. He didn't want Electa doting over him and feeling sorry for him. He wanted her safe and happy and hoped that she was.

Beidler had learned about Plummer's friends and approached James in town. He wanted James to attend an organizational meeting of the Bannack vigilantes, but James refused to have any active part. Since Plummer had known Yeager, James did wonder if there wasn't something to the rumors. But he had known Henry longer than anyone except Joseph, the Vails, and Electa, and felt him to be a man of character. Electa had been right about that. James could even say that he loved Henry like a brother, as he did Joseph. And yet, he also felt a keen responsibility to the people of Bannack. Serious crimes against them had been committed. And then there were the vigilantes, and Beidler's warning not to take the wrong side. And so in the end, he chose the safe path of silence, and his conscience stung because of it.

Since Martha's heart lay heavy with worry for Henry and grief from the loss of Electa's companionship, she wrote her a letter.

My Dearest Electa,   January 9th, 1864

I hope this finds you fair and well. You would never believe the events that have occurred if I was not testimony to them. A band of men have taken it upon themselves to act as lawmen, judges, and "without proper course of law," as Henry puts it. They ignore his authority and position as though he didn't even exist. He refuses to speak of it. I don't know what he is going to do, since Chief Justice Edgerton seems to support their actions, something I cannot understand. His nephew, Sanders, led the awful sham before the mob hung two unfortunate men.

My dear, what is to become of the little civilized society we have, when elected officers of the law like Henry aren't recognized, nor respected? I am beside myself with worry for him, my dear, as well as for you. I tell you of this, not to alarm you, but to inform you of Henry's situation since I'm sure he hasn't told you himself. As always, your loving sister,

Martha

Chapter Twenty Nine ~ An Early End

Sheriff Plummer's trip to Fort Benton to protect Largent and Carroll's gold about did him in. The Vails had insisted that he stay with them at night, so they could help him if need be. His health grew increasingly worse; his voice became hoarse from coughing, his complexion paled, and his frame thinned. James feared that Henry would die before spring unless they could get him to a hospital, but there was none available. Henry hadn't mentioned of leaving to join Electa.

On the evening of January tenth, Francis and Joseph opened their store for awhile. Francis sat in a chair by the stove warming himself while Joseph cleaned up from the day's business. Sidney Edgerton came in and sat down. They talked until Francis had to leave for supper, so Edgerton did the same. Joseph stayed, saying that he wasn't hungry, and that he would eat later. Plummer couldn't eat much, so he took off his gunbelt and set it aside on the parlor floor before lying down on a couch to rest. Francis finished eating and excused himself, saying he was going to attend choir practice at the Edgerton's. It was only a short walk through the cold and snow. Mary opened the door.

"Good evening, Mr. Thompson," she said. "Please come in."

"Hello, Mrs. Edgerton," Francis said stepping inside. "I've come for choir practice." Seeing Mattie and Lucia, he greeted them. He thought they seemed nervous and upset but had no idea why.

"Practice has been canceled tonight," Mary said matter-of-factly and shut the door. She, too, seemed upset, and looked at Sidney, who motioned for Francis to sit down.

"Have a chair, Francis," Edgerton said. "You might as well stay awhile. It's a quiet night, isn't it?" Francis started to ask why the practice had been canceled, but for some reason, perhaps the nervousness of the ladies, he thought better of it.

~

Martha washed the dishes and put the children to bed. When finished, she found Henry asleep in the parlor, a single oil lamp gently throwing its soft yellow glow from a corner table behind a rocking chair. She sat down and read her Bible, thought, and prayed for awhile.

~

The Edgerton women worked in the kitchen and prepared the children for bed. The two men talked for awhile about nothing in particular until they heard the sound of men walking on snow outside. The distinctive crunching of boots on dry snow went on for several minutes, almost alarming Francis.

"Judge," Francis said, "where could all those men be going?"

"I wouldn't worry about affairs that don't concern you," Edgerton said. His rudeness shocked Francis but he wouldn't consider reciprocating by leaving immediately. He decided to wait.

~

At the Vails, someone suddenly knocked on the front door, startling Martha. Henry raised his head and groaned, only half awake.

"I'll get it, Henry," Martha said, "but it's probably for you this time of night." She opened the door to a bitterly cold night and four men.

"Henry Plummer," the man in front said. Hearing his name, Henry sat up and sleepily shook his head. Martha wondered why he hadn't addressed Henry as sheriff. Henry rubbed his eyes to wake up, got up, and went to the door.

"Come with us," the man said.

Henry tied a scarf around his neck, got his coat from beside the door and stepped outside.

"Henry!" Martha cried out. He turned to face her and grinned.

"Go back inside, Martha. They only want to talk to me about Dutch John." Hesitating, she obeyed, reckoning that he knew his business. As the cold air awakened him, he greeted the men he knew while leading them next door to Sanders's. He noticed three things simultaneously: their guns, more men coming out from behind the Vails and Sanders's light go out. He suddenly regretted the fact that he had left his own gun in the Vail's parlor. He stopped in his tracks, twenty feet short of Sanders's door.

"Men," he said, "None of you has yet broken any law that I know of. Where is Dutch John?" The men didn't know what to say and began looking at each other nervously. Suddenly the Sanders's door opened and Sanders stepped outside.

"Company!" he ordered, "Forward march!" It was too dark to see him, but the sheriff recognized his voice. "Sanders!" Henry called out but no answer came. Looking around, he realized that there were at least two dozen armed men around him. The men obeyed Sanders's order and fell in around and behind Plummer, who began to walk again.

~

Alarmed and frightened, Martha donned her coat and ran through the cold night to the Edgerton's as Henry, at the center of the crowd of men, disappeared into the darkness.

"Francis! Francis!" she cried out, her scared voice broken with sobs. She pounded on the door repeatedly until Sidney opened it. Before he could say a word, she saw Francis and rushed in toward him, weeping wildly. "They've taken Henry!" she sobbed.

Mattie and Lucia looked at one another, helpless, and tears welled up in their eyes as they sympathized with the woman. Francis stood with his arms around Martha, patting her on the back. Mary quietly approached them.

"Mrs. Vail," Mary said, "The sheriff is only wanted in town to discuss Dutch John's arrest. I'm sure your fears are unfounded."

After a few moments Martha calmed somewhat.

"Come, Martha, I'll take you home," Francis said. He helped her walk back home through the snow as she wept. There, she sat in the parlor while he made her some tea. His mind raced, wondering about the possible events taking place, and he felt helpless, except for what he could do for Martha.

~

The crowd of men filed across the Grasshopper Creek footbridge, keeping Henry in the midst. For some reason, Henry thought of the morning that he, the Vails, Joseph, and Francis walked Electa across that same bridge the morning she left. As the organized squad fell back into formation and started down Main Street, a larger squad of men joined them. In the cold, clouds of breath puffed from each man's mouth. The only sound was their snow-steps.

Henry saw that they had also taken two of his deputies into custody, Buck Stinson and Ned Ray. He realized that the three of them were about to be accused of great crimes by at least seventy-five men.

"You men know us better than this!" he called out.

"If there is an honest man among you," Buck said, "you'll admit our innocence!"

The scores of armed men continued their silent march down Main Street. Just past the Goodrich, the mob guided their prisoners north to the edge of town and up the low hill to the gallows that Bannack's lawmen had themselves built, and from which they had hung Peter Horan. The first guards to reach the gallows formed a large circle around them. A few gray clouds passed slowly overhead through the black sky, hiding some stars.

"Men, can't you at least give us a trial?" Henry said. The guards directed the three condemned men to the gallows. A simple structure, it consisted of two sturdy upright pine posts, which supported another post across the top. It had room enough for several men at a time.

"Plummer!" Buck said, "They're really going to hang us!" Henry noticed Sanders among the men.

"Henry Tilden," Sanders said. The young man stepped forward, his hands in his pockets.

"Yes, sir, Mr. Sanders," he said.

"Return to the Edgertons for more rope."

"Yes, sir," Tilden said, and hurried away into the darkness.

"My poor wife," Plummer said. "I would like to speak to my sister-in-law. Men, you can't do this without giving us time to settle business accounts. At least my wife has that right," he said, to which there was no reply. "We want a fair trial," he stated loudly and coughed.

"We've already held your trial," a voice from the darkness said, "and the only trial you will have now will be at the end of a rope."

"This isn't justice," Plummer argued. His deputies also hotly protested, but in vain.

"It is useless to beg for your lives," another said. "You are to be hanged."

After several long minutes, Tilden arrived from his errand with the long tool of death looped over his shoulder.

They hung Ned Ray first, holding him up and dropping him. His girl, Madam Hall, tried to reach him by hysterically trying to push through the thick ring of guards, but he kicked his life away while she wept inconsolably, held back by the guards.

"There goes poor Ed Ray," Buck said. Some of the guards conducted the weeping woman back to her cabin.

Buck Stinson was led under the gallows next. The coiled and knotted rope was placed around his neck; several men hoisted him up and roughly dropped him.

It occurred to a few of the guards that it was only the second time that they had seen Plummer agitated. The first was at Jack Cleveland's death. Now Henry stood helpless and without hope. He thought of Electa and his friends, and wondered where Francis and Joseph were.

"Bring up Plummer!" one of the executioners commanded. The sheriff stood his full height, determined to keep his dignity to the end. No man moved. Suddenly a commotion occurred outside the ring of guards.

"Henry!" It was Joseph Swift. "Why are you doing this?" he cried out, striking the guards, sobbing, and trying to prevent his friend's inevitable death.

"Please don't do this!" he cried out and collapsed on the frozen snow-covered ground, blubbering and weeping.

Henry could partly see him through the ring of men. He untied his neck scarf and flung it in Joseph's direction.

"Give this to Joe," he said. It lay on the white snow in a small blue pile.

The commander stepped up and motioned for Plummer's hands to be bound behind his back. Two men slowly came forward. The sheriff stood still as they tied his hands. Each man took one of his arms and led him under the gallows, beside where their second victim, Buck Stinson, hung strangled. The third rope was placed around Henry's neck and the loop tightened. He coughed.

"Give a man time to pray," Henry said and coughed again.

"You're out of time," one of the men said.

"Give me a high drop, boys," Henry said.

Two men took his legs, two others grasped his arms, all lifted as high as they could, and at the same time abruptly dropped him.

~

A short time later, a man called out of the darkness in front of the Vail house, "It's all over!"

In the parlor, Martha sat up in her chair. "What does that mean?" she said, shaken. James sat forward on the couch.

"Martha, it can only mean one thing," he said. She looked at him with wide, scared eyes, her hands clasping the arms of the chair. He wished to be anywhere else on earth than where he was, with almost any other duty. "Martha, I'm afraid that they must have hung Henry." Shock showed on her face. She sighed and fainted, collapsing back into the chair.

He knew that she needed to be revived, but didn't want to face her. Instead, he wanted to find out exactly what had happened. He hesitated, looked at her, decided that she was safe, and left her alone as he ran next door to get Hattie Sanders to help her.

~

The next day, Martha knew that she must write Electa of the unspeakable news.

My Dear Sister,   January 11th, 1864

Never have I regretted having to tell anyone what I must tell you. How I wish that we had never come to this awful, dreadful place! But now I must share the terrible news. Henry has been killed, hung by a mob of men who took him last night, sick and pale though he was. Oh, how I wish I were there with you when you open this alarming and sad letter! They condemned our dear Henry without allowing him so much as a defense. I cannot and shall never believe that he is guilty of the crimes for which he died. Such a kind, noble soul would not have been the leader of a band of thieves. Francis was not there, nor did he suspect any violence until, he said, the deed was probably over and done with. Joseph learned too late of the immoral and cowardly act, and could do nothing to prevent it. My dear sister, may God help you through this awful time. I await the day when we shall again embrace.

Your loving sister,
Martha

Sources and Acknowledgments

Anderson, Linda E. *Bannack* The Bannack Association, Montana Fish, Wildlife and Parks, and The Montana State Parks Interpretive Association, no publishing date.

Dimsdale, Thomas J. *The Vigilantes of Montana* Norman: University of Oklahoma Press, 1953.

Graves, F. Lee *Bannack Cradle of Montana* Helena: American & World Geographic Publishing, 1991.

Judith Basin County Press *John Largent's Story* Thursday, January 7, 1937.

Mather, R.E. & Boswell, F.E. *Hanging the Sheriff: A Biography of Henry Plummer*, Missoula: Historic Montana Publishing, 1987.

McCutcheon, Marc *The Writer's Guide to Everyday Life in the 1800s* Cincinnati: Writer's Digest Books, 1993.

Pace, Dick *Golden Gulch The Story of Montana's Fabulous Alder Gulch* Virginia City: Dick Pace, 1962.

Sargent, Tom *The Civil War in Montana* Internet Article, October 22, 1998.

Copy of Lithograph: U.S.P.R.R. Survey artist drawing 1860 of Fort Benton. Sarony, Major & Knapp Lithographs.

About the Author

Since 1978, Dennis Fabel, his wife Carolyn, a Montana native, and their children have been intermittent Montana residents, having lived in Clinton, Frenchtown, Missoula, and Stevensville. Their last Montana residence was in Sheridan, near Bannack in southwest Montana. They have walked the streets of Bannack many times, and return every year to reflect on Montana's early history and the lives of those who lived there.

Dennis holds a Bachelor of Arts degree from Pacific Coast Baptist Bible College and a Bachelor of Liberal Science degree from the University of Montana, Western. Since 1996, he has been pastor of the First Baptist Church of Sligo, near Wilmington, Ohio.

The Fabels raised four children in Montana, where their son, Will, still lives.